P9-DFU-574

THE HOLDOUTS

Also by William Decker

TO BE A MAN

THE HOLDOUTS

a
novel by
William Decker

LITTLE, BROWN AND COMPANY BOSTON TORONTO

FIRST EDITION

Library of Congress Cataloging in Publication Data

Decker, William.
The holdouts.

I. Title.
PZ4.D2936Ho [PS3554.E195] 813'.5'4 79-13348
ISBN 0-316-17917-5

BC
Published simultaneously in Canada
by Little, Brown & Company (Canada) Limited
PRINTED IN THE UNITED STATES OF AMERICA

For Anne

"What folks can't see they say ain't there. We're here, same as always. Been here all along. Holdouts. Aim to be here a spell longer."

—Jake Scott, 1964

THE HOLDOUTS

1

IT HAD RAINED in the night. A gentle steady rain, and Sam Howard felt the exhilaration that always lifted his spirits when even a little moisture leaked from the sky to dampen the thirsty range in northern Arizona. He pressed his boot against the accelerator and the battered blue pickup responded. A gray ribbon of road stretched out straight ahead toward the western mountains and the land gave off a fresh, just-rained-on aroma as the pickup sped along. Sam had the windows rolled down and he breathed deeply, savoring the odors of settled dust, wet sage, and cedar. This was his country at its best. The vast blue of the sky in front of him was dotted with towering cotton-ball clouds that seemed to hang motionless above the peaks to the west, the ragged badlands to the north, and the flat horizon in the south and east. Three hundred and sixty degrees of sky. It was a good day and great country. Enough to lift any man's spirits, but Sam could not entirely shake off the nameless depression, the vague dissatisfaction, that had gnawed at him all morning.

Shaving, in the harsh fluorescent light, he had raised his concentrated stare from his chin to his eyes and for an instant had seen his father's face looking back at him from the mirror. The impression only lasted a moment, but it unsettled him. From the fine sandy hair above the pale, hat-protected part of the forehead with two wavy grooves across it, to the eyebrows set against darker, weathered skin, the straight nose, the wide mouth with determinedly set lips, and the square chin, it seemed to be his father's face. Especially the eyes. They startled Sam the most. Not in their dark-brown color or their steady gaze. Not even because of the deep lines drawn back from their outside corners, or the slanting folds of skin in the lids, which partially hooded the eyes from above. It was the expression of resignation in the eyes that bothered him. Sam had not expected that. He had always thought of his eyes as reflecting interest and excitement. The ones he saw in the mirror were dull and cautious. Tired.

The moment passed, but the impression stayed with him. Driving from the ranch to town, even the lift he got from the after-smell of rain could not overcome his mood. At forty-four was there nothing for him to look forward to except gradual physical deterioration? Would he spend the rest of his days working for wages and die as his father had, without very much to show for a lifetime of hard work? Was it all downhill from here? There was satisfaction in the work, being foreman of a big, open-range ranch, even the possibility of pride, and that had been enough for his father. But Bob Howard had never known any other ambition or any other life. Sam had. Sam needed more. He had been a competitor all his life, challenging himself, testing his body, his skill, his nerve. Now it seemed that there were no challenges left. All that the future seemed to promise was taking the seasons of the year, and the work that went with them, one after another. No more high spots. No heroics.

Well, he thought, I've left lots of footprints. Maybe it's time I shortened my stirrups and started behaving like I expected to die in bed.

He settled back and guided the pickup with one hand as it swept along, throwing a shadow across the borrow pit that paralleled the road. A thorny lace border of tumbleweeds was tangled against the bottom strand of the barbed-wire fence, and the cedar posts blurred by. Suddenly the fence on the other side of the highway changed color for a stretch of nearly a hundred feet. The new posts were lighter than the old ones, and shiny splices of new wire sparkled in the sun. Sam's wide mouth spread in a wry grin as he squinted at the road ahead. All that he could remember of the accident was the explosion that woke him when his car plowed through the fence, clipping off posts, crack-crack-crack, and the wires screeching through staples as he braked and wrenched the steering wheel. Then the stillness in the moonlight.

In a little while, he mused, those posts will weather, and the new wire will get dull. Not like the gash I put in that big old ponderosa on the ranch road two years ago. That blaze will be a long time healing over. For all the nicks and notches I've left along the way between town and home, it's a wonder I've never really gotten hurt. Took some paint off this old pickup, and had to have a new front end put on the car, but outside of some bumps and bruises I haven't done myself much damage. Just dumb luck.

The shadow of the pickup rippled over the margin of the highway at a great rate, and Sam was reminded of the way the shadow of his damaged P–51 had bounced along just below when he brought it home to England at treetop level. When the engine seized, the shadow rushed up to meet him and merged with the Mustang as it scraped across the tarmac. He remembered watching other shadows. As a boy astride his first horse, Blucher, loping over vast prairies of grama grass, imagining himself stirrup to stirrup with Custer. As a halfback on the Baxter High School football team, running an end sweep and in his mind wearing the jersey of West Point. As a cadet pilot trainee, marching across a macadam airstrip and pretending he was a member of the Lafayette Escadrille. Coming clear of the chutes on a lunging saddle bronc; leaning forward on a long-striding polo pony, cocking his mallet for the next lofting drive; and just recently, riding out to scatter the crew for spring roundup, knowing what he could expect from each of the men and confident of their respect. Perhaps not the cattleman his father had been but sure enough of himself to give others confidence, always measuring up to his own expectations of himself.

A scrapbook of shadows, he was thinking. Reminders. I've been there. As old Jake would say, I've seen the elephant and heard the owl. If I've been a little wild from time to time, it's just because taking chances keeps you from getting bored. Somebody said it once: if you ever get bored with life just go out and risk it. Right. Just go out and risk it.

Sam slowed down as he approached the outskirts of Baxter. Before the highway had been widened and generally improved, there had been an abrupt dip here, just before the sign giving the population and elevation figures, where the pavement dropped to the bottom of a wash. Now it was leveled out with a culvert in the arroyo to handle the infrequent runoff from the mountains. Sam remembered how he and Red Farnsworth would perch on the rocks above the road like a pair of Indians on ambush and wait for unwary tourists who either did not understand or just did not heed the U-shaped sign that warned of the dip. When they spotted an out-of-state car coming, they would crouch behind the rocks until the car hit the depression going too fast, scraped its tail pipe on the bottom, and literally sailed up on the other side. Then the two boys would war-whoop with delight. Now Baxter had spread out along the highway, which was the town's Main Street, but stopped in a cluster of fast-food drive-ins and filling stations just before the arroyo on the east. On the western side of town new developments in the form of garish motels and restaurants with elaborate neon signs stretched farther out into the rangeland. The town itself was six blocks of solid buildings of locally quarried red sandstone or imported brick. In the center was the county courthouse with broad stairs leading up from Main Street. This was Sam's destination. Red Farnsworth, sheriff of Piñon County, had called and left word with Sam's wife, Lucy, that he wanted to see Sam.

"He sure sounded serious, hon," Lucy said, and Sam could tell that she was worried. "You didn't do anything crazy in town the other night, did you?"

"No crazier than usual," Sam said, unwilling to admit that he did not remember much about the last part of that evening. He thought he had simply hung around his favorite bar, The Homestead, talking to the bartenders, Perry and Floyd, and a few old friends. Boots Taylor had been there.

Sam stopped the pickup at the first of the four traffic lights on Main Street and waved to Boots, who was wiping the windshield of an out-of-state car at the pump in front of his gas station. A stocky, bowlegged man, he looked uncomfortable afoot, but he was graceful in the saddle and was always ready when Sam needed extra help for the spring and fall roundups. Sam grinned remembering how last year Red Farnsworth had gently but unmistakably warned Boots that too many tourists, who stopped at Boots's station, were discovering that their alternators were on the verge of shorting out. Not wanting to find themselves stranded miles from help, the travelers usually allowed Boots to replace the part with a bargain-priced "rebuilt" unit. Red suggested that Boots would do well to give up this profitable sideline, and Boots agreed, the way most people did when Red made suggestions.

"That big bastard don't miss a trick," Boots told Sam. "How in hell do you suppose he found out I was working the pilgrims for a few bucks? Damned if he don't beat all. Oh well, it was knuckle-busting work anyway. Taking out those things and scrubbing them with solvent and putting them back in. I won't miss it."

The traffic light changed, and Sam shifted gears without haste because he knew that the lights were timed so that he would have to stop at each of them. This was a deliberate arrangement, designed to keep traffic speed down on Main Street and to give transients every chance to look the town over and perhaps stop to spend a little money. Baxter was "town" for all of the loggers, ranchers, Indians and miners for miles in every direction. Most of them came to town infrequently, but when they did, they bought truckloads of supplies and made the trip an occasion. To them Baxter was a place and an attitude of mind. Going into town was physical and geographical. Going to town was what you did when you got there. Home was where you went afterwards. Home could be a definite, permanent place, or the most transitory kind of camp. It was a location where there was some degree of security. It was where you were when you were not in town. Home and town were both real and metaphoric.

Since Baxter was a fairly old town, as western towns go, and the county seat, certain long-established policies prevailed. Discreet prostitution and quiet gambling were tolerated by the authorities because they had been part of the town since its beginning as a nameless railroad camp, and because they were considered necessities. There were two well-run whorehouses, each catering to a distinct clientele, which served the social, as well as the sexual, needs of the men who came to Baxter—a man could drop by for only a drink and conversation if he wished. Each house was assessed by the town fathers according to its volume of business, and every Monday morning the madams deposited their fee in account number 308 at the Baxter National Bank. This account was drawn upon by the county commissioners for civic improvements. The existence of the establishments north of the railroad tracks, which ran parallel to Main Street, was largely ignored by the local clergy and church members, and only a few officials were aware of account 308. The cowboys and loggers spent most of their time on the north side of town, where the rules were more relaxed than they were in the business and residential sections to the south. The arrangement worked very well.

Sam parked in back of the courthouse and climbed the stone stairway to the second floor, where a polished brass plate on a wooden door said SHERIFF'S OFFICE. Red Farnsworth was listening to the telephone and writing on a lined pad of yellow paper as Sam entered. Red looked up and nodded toward a sturdy chair of well-worn oak. Sam sat down, lit up a Lucky, and studied the big man behind the desk. Everything about Red was massive. Everything from his square-tipped, sausage-shaped fingers to his long lobed ears, which thrust out below the thatch of dark red hair he had never been able to subdue with comb or brush. Sam remembered that when they were boys, Red had secretly used some of his mother's sewing machine oil on his hair in an effort to make it lie flat.

"OK," Red said into the phone. "Keep me posted."

He turned toward Sam as he hung up.

"Damndest thing," the big man said. "That was the state police. They got a bulletin from Nevada about a pair of escaped convicts who have been working their way south holding up whorehouses. They're armed, but they haven't shot anybody yet. Knocked over five that reported it. Maybe more that didn't."

"Headed our way?" Sam asked.

"According to our guys, Nevada thinks they may be in Vegas."

"Well," Sam said, "if I was on the lam, I'd feel a lot less conspicuous in that twenty-four-hour mob scene in Vegas than I would down here in Baxter. Strangers get noticed here."

"You can't ever tell," Red said glancing at a large map on the wall. "They could just as easy turned off west for California. Let me put this make on their car on the bulletin board."

Red strode out with the yellow pad in his left hand, and Sam noticed that his right hand rested for a moment on the checkered grip of the .44 Magnum that rode in its holster. Sam remembered when Red had received the big pistol four years ago, in 1960.

"Ain't it a dandy," Red had said as he wiped the

gleaming blue-black weapon with an old undershirt.

"Christ, Red, what do you want with a cannon like that? The damn thing is a foot long."

"Eleven and seven-eighths inches. Here, heft it."

Sam took the pistol and was surprised at its weight. He turned it from side to side, studying the massive frame and long, ribbed barrel. Even unloaded it felt as though it would be hard to hold at arm's length for long. Sam raised it and sighted at the window across the room.

"It sure is big," he said. "And heavy."

"Has to be," Red said. "It's got a helluva recoil. But this isn't the biggest one they make. This has the six-and-a-half-inch barrel. They make one with a barrel over eight inches. I figured that might get to be unhandy."

"What's the matter with the old forty-five?"

"Nothing really. This one hits harder. It's good for shooting cars. You can stop one with this. It's got more punch than that thirty-thirty." Red nodded toward the rifle cabinet across the room.

"Do me a favor," Sam said. "Let me know when you get ready to use that thing. I want to be standing way behind you."

Red came back into the room and lowered his bulk into the unpadded oak swivel chair at his desk.

"OK, Sam," he said, picking up a typewritten letter, "here's why I called. A brand inspector down south in Pima County filed a report on fifteen head of yearling steers that came into an auction yard there with worked-over brands. He had them impounded, and when they clipped the hair and got a good look at the brands, the steers turned out to be your stock. He says that the original iron was a Rocking R."

"Sonofabitch," Sam muttered and stood up.

"He says here that somebody who didn't know how to use a running iron had tried to convert the Rocking R into a wagon wheel by bringing the rocker clear around into a circle with the round part of the R as the hub of the wheel and the legs of the R as spokes. They burned in the extra spokes."

"I'll be damned," Sam said reaching for the letter.

"The problem is," Red went on, "while they were getting a better look at the steers, whoever brought them to the auction made tracks. Nobody remembers much about him. He was long gone when they went to look for him."

Sam read the letter scowling. He could not accept what it so plainly said.

"Of course," Red said, "the big question is, were those fifteen head all that were stolen or just the ones they did a bad job of altering the brands on. If they got away with a whole slug of steers, they could be feeding out the rest of them if they figure the brands are good enough to pass. These fifteen could be just the ones they got nervous about and decided to dump quick."

"Spencer Butterfield is going to have a hemorrhage," Sam said.

"Don't you know it. He goes on the fight if anybody even mentions rustlers. I'll never forget him coming by after I got elected in forty-five. Right in this room. He shook my hand and said, 'Don't waste your time on things that don't matter, but put the fear of God into the cow thieves. Let them know that this county is unhealthy.' He meant it, too. That's one thing he won't tolerate. One time I tried to explain to him how hard it was to get a conviction unless you actually caught a rustler in the act. He didn't want to hear about it. Kept shaking his head. Told me if I ever had the goods on a cow thief and couldn't get the court to lock him up, to let him know. He said he had men down in Mexico on the Magdalena Ranch who knew how to handle rustlers. He'd send them up. I bet he would, too."

"He's going to have a third-degree fit," Sam said. "Has anybody around here reported any stock stolen?"

"Not recently. A couple of years ago I had some complaints about missing calves, but that stopped after I had a talk with a certain party."

"Ted Beemer?"

Red nodded. "But this is too big a deal for him. He'll steal a calf out of somebody's pasture, but not a truckload of steers. How many steers are you running?"

"Three thousand and some."

"All natives?"

"Yeah. Butterfield said he wasn't going to send any *corrientes* up from Magdalena this year, so we held over most of the steer calves last fall along with the replacement heifers."

"Where are you carrying them?"

"The steers are all up in the Bill Williams country. The heifers are down on Elk Creek," Sam said.

"How in hell could anybody get in and out of that Bill Williams range?" Red asked.

"There's just no way," Sam said, shaking his head. "There's rimrock and badlands all across the north end and the river to the west. The only way in from the south is the road right by headquarters, and even if they could find a way in from the east, the only roads over there go past two line camps with men in them. Men who would be sure to notice. Old Jake Scott is up at the summer camp, and Martin Yazzi, the Indian, is in the Bill Williams pasture camp. You'd never get by either of them. They ride their country, and they read sign."

Sam squinted toward the window and frowned.

"I'm going to have to get a tally on those steers," he said quietly. "I'm going to have to find out how many are missing."

"How long do you figure it will take?"

"Depends on how soon I can get a crew up there. A week if I can find some good men," Sam said.

"I could ask the Forest Service for a plane," Red said, "or a helicopter. We could do it quicker that way."

Sam shook his head. "We'll do it horseback and do it right. I want to put them through a gate and see each one; not guess at how many are lying up in the brush."

"For a guy that flew fighters in the war, you sure don't seem to have much use for airplanes," Red said with a grin.

"Planes are good for a lot of things," Sam said, "but

counting cattle isn't one of them. You can fly around and get an idea of what range conditions are, or if cattle are ganging up in an area. But this needs men on horses."

Red nodded. "I didn't figure you would go for the idea. I just thought I would try to get that rawhide outfit you run out there a little bit up to date."

"Sure," Sam said, frowning, "but this has got to be done right, or I may not be running that rawhide outfit much longer."

He turned away and stared out the window. How in God's name could anyone have stolen those steers? Here it is 1964 and that age-old problem is still around. Butterfield will blow a gasket. According to the stories, the old man had won his war with the rustlers in Mexico by arming his men and telling them to shoot first and ask questions later. But this is 1964. You can't go around shooting people the way they used to. Besides, with over seven hundred thousand acres to protect, more than a thousand square miles of rugged country called the Rocking R, how could you cover it all? Yes, it was a rawhide outfit all right. Butterfield had seen to that, and as it turned out, the old man's theories had been right. But now this. Rustlers!

The telephone rang, and Red answered it. He listened a moment and said, "I'm on my way." He shoved the receiver back in its cradle and rose. "Come on," he said, as Sam stood up. "They're sticking up Mattie's place." Red lifted the carbine from the gun cabinet and was through the door in three strides with

Sam right behind him. In the car Red drove urgently but without using the siren. They went north on Third Street, across Main and the railroad tracks, and turned east on Front Street. Instead of going to the corner of First Street, where Mattie's big stone house stood, Red turned at Second and then into the alley. He stopped the car and thrust the carbine at Sam.

"I'm going in the back. You go around and watch the front door. Just show them that piece, don't use it."

Sam nodded, and the steel of the carbine chilled his hands. As Red went around the garage one way, he went the other and slipped between it and the tall chain link fence surrounding the bottled-gas dealer's lot next door. Just show it to them, don't use it, he was thinking. What the hell do you do if you show it to them and they keep on coming? He came to the front of the big house and climbed the stone steps to the door with its panel of frosted glass. Now what? Maybe I should back off, get down on the sidewalk so they can see the carbine before they run smack into it. He hesitated, and as he did, a gun went off inside the house. He flung himself against the door, which turned out to be unlocked and opened easily. Inside it was dark, and he ducked to one side instinctively. He heard Red saying something from beside the stairway, and then his eyes were adjusted, and he saw the body at the foot of the stairs.

"Just come on down slow," Red said, and Sam watched a small man with his hands up come carefully down the carpeted stairs. "Nice and easy," Red said, and the little man came toward the large one a step at a time. The man sprawled at the bottom of the stairs did not move; a pistol lay in the corner pointed toward the baseboard. Red handcuffed the small man and searched him thoroughly, discovering a switch-blade knife and a flat automatic pistol. He pocketed these and led his prisoner to a couch and sat him down.

"Sam, call my office and tell Jerry to come on over," Red said. "OK, Mattie," he called up the stairs, "it's all over."

Sam heard voices from upstairs as he dialed, and when he hung up he saw Mattie stepping around the body at the foot of the stairway. She was dressed for town in a blue gabardine dress with a white belt. A tall shapely woman with black hair, who always moved in a graceful way that called attention to her figure, she came to Red and pressed her cheek to his chest.

"Christ, I was scared," she whispered.

Red reached around and gently placed his huge hands over her shoulder blades.

"No wonder," he said and looked toward the front door as the sound of a siren came toward them.

"Here comes that silly sonofabitching Jerry. Best we open the door, or he'll break it down," Red said.

Brakes screeched, and the siren died with a moan. Sam opened the door as Jerry reached the porch. He was a small wiry man in a sharply pressed tan uniform with his Stetson cocked low over his right eye. His hand was curled around the butt of a single-action Colt in a carved holster on his thigh.

"Hot damn!" he exclaimed when he saw the body in the hall. "You got him. Why didn't you call me, Red?"

"No time," Red said. "Here's his partner."

Red gestured at the man seated on the couch, and Jerry spun toward him. The second robber was even smaller than Jerry, and the deputy drew himself up to stand as tall as he could in his high-heeled boots.

"You take the stiff over to Jansen's," Red ordered, "while Sam and I take this one in and book him."

Jerry nodded, and Sam moved to help him carry the corpse to the patrol car in front of the house. When he came back, Red was comforting Mattie, and the girls upstairs were chattering. The prisoner was sitting forward on the couch with his hands behind his back. Sam studied the small man's face but could detect no sign of emotion, just resignation and defeat.

"Your luck ran out, pal," Sam said, and the small man only shrugged.

"What happened?" Sam asked when they were back in Red's office.

"Well, I came in the back way and started for the stairs. The girl who called said that they had everybody in a bedroom up there. She had managed to slip out somehow. Anyway, as I was coming alongside the stairs, the taller one started down. All I could see at first were his feet. Just then you came to the front door, and I saw your silhouette on the glass. When I looked back up, I saw a gun and figured you were about to get shot, so I didn't have time to do anything but poke my pistol up and blast. He never knew what hit him."

"Sweet Jesus," Sam whispered.

"I don't much like it, but I didn't have any choice," Red said quietly. "The gun was leveling right on you. He was above me, out of reach. Nothing I could do."

Sam reached out and gripped Red's thick forearm. They had known one another so well for so long that words were not needed. Sam knew that Red had often taken risks to avoid using a gun. He was tough, but not sadistic. He could be very rough, but not mean. Somewhere along the line he had developed a sense of honor and a probity he was determined to measure up to, come what may. Sam knew that even when they had been boys in high school, Red's integrity was far stronger than his own. It had always been Sam who suggested playing hooky, who came up with the pranks that sometimes got them both in trouble. It had been Sam who always seemed to get into fights, and Red who settled them. With his size and strength, Red had always been a formidable fistfighter, but he tried to avoid fighting. Sam remembered how disturbed Red had been when an old logger had given them advice on how to fight. They had been at a dance when a fight broke out in the parking lot and a crowd gathered to watch two men slug it out in a clearing among the cars and pickups. No rowdiness or drinking was allowed inside the community dance hall, so it all took place out in the parking lot, and this was the third fight that night. It ended when one of the men went down and did not rise again. Sam had been awed by the solid blows the men exchanged. The sight of grown men battling was so much grimmer than boys wrestling in the schoolyard. But the old logger standing beside them shook his head and spat in disgust.

"Don't know a damn thing about fighting anymore," he said. "Knock a man down and the fight's over. Hell, that's when you want to go to work on him. Put him in bed for a week or two so he can think over how bad you beat him. Kick him! Stomp on him! Give him the logger's smallpox."

"Logger's smallpox?" Sam asked.

"Yeah," the old man growled. "Walk all over him with your calked boots. Leave some marks for him to remember you by."

Walking home that night Sam laughed and waved his arms. "*Kick* him! *Stomp* on him!" he shouted. "Give him the logger's smallpox! Oh boy, oh boy."

"I could never kick a man who's down," Red said. "It's just not right."

"Well, you want to stay out of the timber then," Sam said, " 'cause that's how they fight in the woods."

"It's going to make trouble," Red was saying.

"What is?"

"The shooting. Church people have been looking for an excuse to close down the whorehouses. Now they'll say they cause crime."

"Christ, Red," Sam said, "we've always had them, and the church people have always wanted to close them down. This isn't going to change anything."

"Maybe not, but it'll stir things up. The usual bunch. They don't seem to understand that this is town for a helluva hunk of territory. It's town to a lot more people than the ones who live in it. If we close the houses, we'll have all the girls on the streets."

"You're really worried, aren't you?"

"Oh, I don't know," Red said. "I guess I'm kind of upset. The shooting. Those bums scaring the hell out of Mattie. Those steers of yours turning up down south."

The telephone rang and Red picked it up. "Yeah. OK, send him up." He hung up and turned back to Sam. "An Indian boy is getting out today, and I want to talk to him before he goes home."

"Do you want me to make myself scarce?" Sam asked.

"No, no. It won't take a minute."

Sam walked to the window and gazed down into the parking lot. When Red answered a knock at the door, Sam turned and saw a slender, dark-haired boy enter the room. Red put his big hand on the boy's shoulder and brought him toward the desk.

"All right, Leon," Red said. "You're on your own now. Do yourself a favor and see if you can't control that temper of yours."

Leon nodded.

"When you get home, tell Jimmy Anderson I want to talk to him. Tell him to come on in and see me, will you?"

Leon nodded again. "Can I have my knife back?" he said.

"Not now," Red said. "You stay out of trouble without it for a while, and we'll see."

"Can I go now?"

"Sure."

The boy left the room, and Red closed the door behind him.

"Is that smart," Sam asked, "sending word that you're looking for Jimmy? Won't he hide out on you?"

"No," Red said. "Jimmy knows I want to talk to him. He knows he's in a little bit of trouble, and he knows he'll be in a lot of trouble if he doesn't come on in and see me. If he comes in now, maybe we can settle things. He'll come in."

2

SAM PARKED HIS PICKUP in front of The Homestead and mounted the high curb to the sidewalk. As he stepped out of the bright sunlight into the dim interior, he was momentarily blinded. He was aware of two men at the end of the bar near the entrance, and he smelled the familiar yeasty aroma of the place. As his eyes adjusted, he glanced up at the mounted heads of high-antlered mule deer and ebony-horned antelope above the ornate backbar. In the middle of the row was the head of a buffalo, massive in its shagginess and dull with dust. The racks of horns were poised and elegant, but occasional cobwebs and the lifeless staring eyes combined to create an effect of ornate decay. The animals seemed to be trying to give the impression that they were not listening to any conversation that might take place at the bar below; they gazed ahead at nothing in the distance. The backbar was all scrolls and columns of dark wood framing tall mirrors and extended far into the deep narrow room. Beyond the far end of the bar was a round card table of yellow oak surrounded by chairs with straight backs. And beyond that was a pool table with thick stubby legs and a neat triangle of colored balls on brushed green felt. Two inverted tulips of multicolored glass hung above the pool table with strong light bulbs nestled inside. A rack against the back wall was filled with cue sticks.

Sam nodded at the two men at the front of the bar and ambled toward the rear where a pudgy man wearing a long white apron was polishing glasses.

"Well," Perry Jefferson said, putting down glass and towel to shake hands with Sam, "didn't expect to see you so soon, but you're just in time to help me choke down my first drink of the day."

Perry turned and looked up at the Western Union clock above the elaborately scrolled cash register, as if he needed confirmation that it was indeed time for a drink. As he tipped his head back, Sam saw the round bald spot in his glistening black hair. Perry put a bottle and two shot glasses on the bar.

"You pour," he said. "I'm a little shaky until I get that first one in me."

Sam poured the bourbon three quarters of the way up each glass.

"Cheers," Perry said, and Sam nodded as they raised the glasses and drank.

"Ah," Perry said, "that's better. Needed that."

He picked up the dish towel and resumed polishing the already gleaming glasses.

"Is Floyd around?" Sam asked.

"Yeah. He'll be coming on soon," Perry said. "I went back and woke him a while ago. He ought to have himself pulled together by now."

"I'm going to need him for a few days, if you can spare him," Sam said. "I've got to gather some steers and get a count on them. Have to collect a crew in a hurry."

"Sure," Perry said nodding. "Old Floyd loves to get out there and cook for your gang. He's still talking about the spring roundup. I guess it takes him back to when he was a hand. Before that bronc made a cook out of him."

"Well, he's one helluva roundup cook, I'll tell you," Sam said. "One of the best I've ever eaten after."

"Go on back and see if he's on his feet," Perry said.

"We had a little excitement this morning," Sam said and went on to describe the holdup at Mattie Mahoney's place. Perry listened intently.

"Sonofabitch," he said. "Old Red just shoved that big gun up that guy's pants leg and touched off a round, did he? How about that. I heard a siren a while ago, but didn't pay much attention."

"That was Jerry," Sam said. "We called him after it was all over to take the stiff to the undertaker's, and here he came with the siren going full blast."

Perry laughed. "He really likes to play that thing. One time I saw him arrest a drunk out at the fairgrounds, and he blew that damn siren all the way into town. Why in hell he does it I don't know. I guess it makes him feel important."

Sam nodded and made his way past the ponderous pool table to a door in the back wall. It led into a narrow hall that was lit by a bare bulb hanging from the ceiling. He passed the door to the storeroom with its thick hasp and heavy padlock, and knocked twice on the next door.

"I'm coming. I'm coming. Hold your water," said a familiar squeaky voice from behind the door.

"It's Sam Howard, Floyd."

The door opened wide and revealed a small man with a large red nose. He was wearing a freshly laundered white shirt with the cuffs of the sleeves turned under and dark slacks that were shiny from wear. "It's just what's above the bar that matters," Floyd always said when Sam teased him about his worn pants. "The apron covers the rest."

"Christ, Sam, come in. I thought you were Perry come after me." He stepped back, and Sam entered the small windowless room. A large brass bed and a badly painted dresser filled most of the space. On top of the dresser was an almost empty bourbon bottle. Floyd saw Sam notice the bottle, and he reached for it.

"One more little touch and I'll be all set," Floyd said and took a gulp that finished the bottle. He coughed and dropped the empty bottle in the wastebasket. It clanked against another bottle at the bottom.

"Awful stuff," Floyd said with a grimace. "Reminds me of the time I picked up a hitchhiker. This feller pulls a pint out of his coat pocket and offers it to me. I said no thanks, and the next thing I know he's dug a big old six-shooter out of his other pocket and the business end is pointing my way. He shoves the bottle at me again, and I got the idea, so I took a swallow.

Well, I'll tell you, that was the roughest stuff I ever layed a lip over. I mean it must have been half paint remover. I choked and wheezed, and my eyes began to leak. 'Christalmighty,' I managed to gasp, 'that's awful. How the hell do you drink it?' 'It ain't easy,' the stranger says and shoves the gun at me butt first. 'You hold the gun on me and I'll try.' "

Sam grinned at the end of the familiar yarn. "You and I could take turns holding a gun on each other," he said, "if you're willing to handle the chuck wagon again for me as soon as I can rustle up a crew."

"Roundup?" Floyd said. "Already?"

"We've got to get a count on the yearling steers in the Bill Williams country," Sam said. "A brand inspector down south says some of our steers went through an auction yard with doctored brands on them. I have to find out how many we're missing."

Floyd pursed his lips in a silent whistle.

"It won't take as long as a regular gather," Sam said. "We'll just have to shove them all down into the bull pasture and get a count on them coming back. With luck it should only take about a week. Are you game?"

"Oh, hell yes," the little man said. "I'll get that same wino pot-walloper that helped me on the branding—old Dave. He's in jail right now, but if I promise Red that we're going clear up in the Bill Williams country where it would take Dave a year to find his way out, Red'll let me borrow him. Save the county having to feed him."

"Good," Sam said. "If you see any likely-looking hands in here, tell them we start Saturday and it's worth ten dollars a day and chuck. You don't need to tell them who's doing the cooking."

"Hell," Floyd said, "I ain't lost a customer yet. You ever hear of anybody walking out on my cooking? No, sir. Of course, we're generally way back up above the first fork in the creek where the owls mate with the chickens, but I suppose somebody could walk out if they were a mind to."

"Come pour me a drink," Sam said. "I'll be your first customer."

"Don't mind if I do," Floyd said. "It's time."

A tall, very slender man wearing a battered straw cowboy hat came through the door from the street. He nodded at the two men near the door and came halfway down the bar toward where Sam stood talking to Perry and Floyd. Perry moved up to wait on the newcomer while Floyd tied on a long white apron.

"Howdy. What can I get you?" Perry said, with a smile that showed flashes of gold.

"Early Times," the stranger said, putting a folded bill on the darkly gleaming bar.

Perry reached back with one hand for a bottle from the row in front of the mirror and at the same time produced a heavy shot glass from beneath the bar. He brought the bottle and the glass together in midair, pouring as he presented them to the new customer. The shot glass was brimful of amber whiskey when it touched the bar. Perry put down the half-full bottle with its silvery spout and drew a small glass of water, which he put next to the shot of whiskey.

"Good booze," Perry said, nodding his head of sleek black hair.

"Have one yourself?" the tall cowboy asked.

Perry twisted his thick body and glanced up at the clock. "Don't mind if I do," he said, as Sam knew he would, no matter what the clock said. Sam had never known Perry to refuse a drink.

Perry produced another shot glass and poured with a steady hand. The liquor reached the brim and bulged on the lip.

"The only time I ever said no was when they asked me if I'd had enough," Perry said, raising his glass toward the customer. "Cheers."

"Luck," the tall man said, and they both drank.

"Ah," Perry said. "Real good booze."

He refilled both shot glasses.

Sam watched, wondering how many million times he had seen this ritual performed. People may think I drink a lot just because I go on a tear now and again, but Perry and Floyd drink all day every day. I'll have a couple of belts in the evening before supper and from time to time take on a snootful here in town, but these two are on the sauce steadily. Well, I guess that's one way to avoid a hangover. Just don't ever sober up.

"You know anything about a cowboy named Sam Howard?" the tall man asked Perry.

Sam did not turn his head, but he tried to get a better look at the face beneath the worn straw hat in the mirror behind the bar.

"Don't know anything good about him," Perry said

trying to scowl and make his round, amiable face look stern.

"He's from around here," the cowboy said. "The Rocking R. I used to rodeo with him."

"Hank Ivy!" Sam said aloud and stepped toward the taller man with his hand outstretched. "You old sonofabitch."

"Sam?" Hank said. "Damn if it ain't."

Perry beamed and brought Sam's glass up beside his and Hank's and refilled them all as Sam and Hank shook hands vigorously.

"What in hell are you doing here?" Sam asked.

"Just passing through," Hank said and grinned, showing long snuff-stained teeth. "Still going down the road looking for rodeos."

"You're still at it?" Sam asked, shaking his head.

"Yeah. I guess the only way they're ever going to make me quit is to cut my head off and bury it where I can't find it."

"But you're not still riding bulls."

"Oh, yeah. I never got any smarter, just stubborner."

"Christ," Sam said. "Some mornings I don't even feel up to riding a gentle horse, and you're still contesting."

"Well," Hank said, "some *mornings* I don't feel so red-hot myself, but by afternoon I get limbered up. Anyhow I'd go crazy staying in one place. Going down the road gets to be a habit. I been doing it so long I can't seem to quit. How long has it been since you quit?"

"It was just after Pendleton in forty-eight," Sam

"Say," he said, rousing himself, "have you got some time? I mean a few days? Can you come out to the ranch for a while?"

"That's what I'm here for," Hank said. "I listened to you talk about the outfit so much I made my mind up to see it someday, and here I am."

"Great," Sam said. "We're going to make a big gather, and we'll see lots of country. I'll make you earn your keep."

"Whoa, now." Hank raised a long-fingered hand. "Remember, I'm an arena cowboy. I don't know anything about ranch cowboying. I'm no brushpopper like you."

"Nothing to it," Sam said, putting some money on the bar. "I'll see you later, Perry. Floyd, you come on out with Boots on Saturday. Bring anybody else you think can stand it."

"Leave your car here while I do a few chores," Sam told Hank as they stepped out into the bright sunlight. "Then we'll head for home."

They got into Sam's pickup. He backed it up and swung it through a U-turn across Main Street and into Boots Taylor's filling station. Boots was peering up at the underside of a car raised high on the grease rack as Sam and Hank walked toward him. Bending back exaggerated his ample belly and made his short, bowed legs look even more out of proportion. He turned to greet Sam, who introduced Hank and explained that the Rocking R steers were going to have to be counted.

"Sure," Boots said in his surprisingly high voice. "You can count me in. My father-in-law can run the station for a few days."

"Ask around and see how many of the guys that helped out in the spring roundup can come," Sam said. "Rusty and Kevin will want to come. I guess you can forget about the Bettencourt kid. He turned out to be as useless as tits on a bull. See if Charlie Grimes is around."

"No, Charlie's watching for fires this summer," Boots said. "But don't worry. I'll get a crew together. We'll be out Saturday afternoon."

Sam and Hank got back in the pickup and drove west on Main Street.

"So this is Baxter, Arizona," Sam said. "Altitude 5,151 feet, population 3,304. Founded back in 1882 as a division terminal of the railroad. It had just been a sort of settlement before that. A camp. They told us in school that it was named for a miner who came in here back in the 1850's and made a helluva strike. Put the place on the map with the rush it caused. There's still some mining going on, but it doesn't amount to much. Fred Harvey built a big hotel here in 1883, and a sawmill got going a few years later. The town has had its ups and downs, but it's the county seat and a steady sort of place. Red Farnsworth is the sheriff and my oldest friend. He runs the county about as honestly as it can be run. Red was a Marine platoon sergeant in the Pacific in World War II. He got wounded and mustered out. He ran for sheriff in 1945 and got elected and has been sheriff ever since. You couldn't live up to whatever image we have of ourselves, or what we think the world expects of us. Dad taught me what to expect of myself, according to his lights. He had contempt for weakness. He was harder on himself than on anyone else. He had to show himself he was what they call a good man. If he had wanted a gravestone, that's what he would have had carved on it. "A Good Man." I guess he got those principles from his father, and felt bound to pass them on to me. I just had to try to live up to what he expected. Sometimes I wonder if that's important anymore. In the old days you had to be tough. You had to be self-reliant because there was nobody else to rely on. Now we've made a virtue out of what started as a necessity. But what would I do if I had a son? Would I tell him that it's all right to cry? Would I let him give up if something got too hard for him to handle? Could I? I'd probably make him tough it out, and be a man.

"I've got to pick up some horseshoe nails," Sam said as he parked in front of the hardware store. "Anything you need?"

"No," Hank said, "but don't count on me to shoe any horses. I'm a bull rider. Remember?"

"We're going to pay a call on a fellow named Ted Beemer," Sam said. He turned north off Main Street and crossed the railroad tracks. "He's got a little place up here in the woods. You might say he's our local desperado. His father came here back during prohibition and was the local bootlegger. Ted went to school with me and Red, and he was always in trouble. We grew up together, and we know what to expect from one another. If there's anybody around here who knows anything about those steers of mine that were stolen, it'll be Ted."

"You think he took them?"

"No. Neither does Red. Ted's a penny-ante kind of thief, but he might know something that I could use. He might have some notion of how it was done."

Sam drove north to the end of the paved road, and turned west on a bumpy track across a sagebrush flat. The rutted road began to climb, and soon they started to pass twisted juniper trees and jack pines. As the road went higher, the trees grew taller, and then they were in the big pines which rose from dark-brown duff shading out the possibility of undergrowth. Deep in the forest they came abruptly upon a ramshackle house in a clearing cluttered with junk. The house gave the impression that it had been assembled haphazardly, over a long period of time, from disparate elements. The front was made of overlapping clapboard with a sagging porch attached to it. One side consisted of a bullet-shaped metal house trailer that looked as though it had rammed into the house and stuck there. The other side was built of unpeeled pine logs and had a long sloping roof covered with tarpaper. There were no windows in that side, and the windows in the center part of the house had sheets of plastic wrap taped to them. The yard was littered with rusting metal drums, gaping engineless car bodies, rolls of Highway Department snow fence, and a wide variety of cannibalized machinery parts. A large

German shepherd dog rushed from the porch through the jumble of junk barking savagely.

"We'll just sit here until somebody comes out," Sam said and lit a cigarette.

The dog stopped ten feet from the pickup and barked steadily. The fur on its neck bristled and long yellow teeth showed beneath its drawn-up lips.

"Yeah," Hank said, "that's one mean-looking puppy."

The front door of the house was thrown open, and a cascade of children poured out. There were seven of them. The smallest was a towheaded boy of about five who ran to the big dog and kicked it in the stomach. The dog stopped barking and slunk under the porch. The little boy laughed and came to join the other children beside the pickup.

"Hi, Sam," the tallest boy said, hitching up his patched Levi's. "Pa's out back."

Sam opened the door and stepped down to the sandy yard. The children stared at him in silence. The little boy who had kicked the dog swaggered toward him.

"I'm Billy," the child said emphatically.

"I know you are," Sam said. "Billy Beemer. I saw your picture in the post office. 'Billy Beemer,' it said, 'Wanted Dead or Alive.' "

The little boy looked puzzled and the other children giggled as Sam looked toward the corner of the house where a small man wearing a leather apron had appeared. Hank joined Sam as they picked their way through the obstacles of rusty metal. Ted Beemer watched them approach. His expression reminded Sam of a weasel because of his narrow face and close-set eyes. The eyes were dark brown, and they shifted nervously from Sam to Hank and back again. Sam was taller than Beemer, and Hank towered over both of them despite his slouch.

"Hi, Ted," Sam said. "How's it going?"

"All right," Beemer said without enthusiasm.

"This is Hank Ivy," Sam said. "An old rodeo buddy of mine." Both men nodded. "He came for a visit, but I'm going to put him to work. We've got to gather our yearling steers, Ted. Are you looking for a few days' work?"

Beemer pushed one hand through his long brown hair and peered at Sam. "Why the hell you gathering steers this time of year?" he asked.

"Red tells me fifteen head with our iron on them turned up at an auction yard in Pima County. I need to find out how many we're missing," Sam said.

"I be go to hell," Beemer said. "How'd anybody ever manage that?"

"Dunno, Ted. You got any notion?"

Beemer glanced up into Sam's eyes. His lips began to twist into a sneer. "So that's it, is it," he said in a low voice. "The minute anything's missing you come snooping around to ask me what I know about it. I'm surprised that big sonofabitching sheriff buddy of yours didn't beat you to it. He's always on my ass. Shit!"

Beemer spat in the sand and looked away.

"No," he said slowly, "I don't know anything about your goddamn steers, and I'm too busy to help you count them."

"Come on, Ted," Sam said. "I know you didn't take

them. I just wondered if you'd seen any unfamiliar trucks on the back roads, or anything."

Beemer shook his head. "No. I ain't seen nothing. Now I got work to do."

"OK, Ted," Sam said, "but if you change your mind come on out Saturday. It pays ten dollars a day and chuck."

Sam and Hank got in the pickup and drove back the way they had come.

"You really want that guy out there working for you?" Hank asked.

"He's a good hand," Sam said. "He knows cattle. Besides, what could he do with all of us there watching?"

"I guess you'd rather have him inside the tent peeing out than outside peeing in, huh?"

"Something like that," Sam said. "I can't really blame Ted for getting sore. As far back as I can remember, people around here have been suspicious of him. Red rides him pretty hard, and that must be tough to take. I wouldn't want Red on my back. Isn't that a great gang of kids he's got? We put on a junior rodeo awhile back, and that oldest boy really showed his stuff. I tried giving him some pointers and told him he could work for me next summer if he wanted to. I like to have a youngster on the crew. I've got a boy out there now, but he says he's going to sign up and go to Vietnam just as soon as he turns eighteen, in October. Will Michaels is his name. He's a wild one. Came out here from West Virginia to learn to cowboy before he goes off to Vietnam to kill people."

"You got any kids?" Hank asked quietly.

"No," Sam said. "Lucy's never got pregnant. The doctor can't explain it. There doesn't seem to be anything physically wrong with either of us."

"That's too bad."

"For Lucy, I guess," Sam said, "but she's come to terms with it. Me, I'm not sure I'd know how to raise kids. I don't have the convictions my father did. I wouldn't know what to tell them."

"Maybe that's the best way to raise them," Hank said. "Leave them alone and let them figure things out as they go along. Tell me something. How did you feel when you quit rodeoing?"

"I didn't miss it much," Sam said. "Oh, I guess I did for a little while, but that didn't last. I used to like the idea of being a double-tough bronc rider. I liked the way it felt when I really got with a horse and took control." He pushed his hat back and grinned his wide grin at Hank. "Nowadays I do my best to talk a horse out of bucking. But once in a while, every now and then, when some old pony gets cranky and thinks it would be a good idea to shed me, I'll just take a deep seat and give him a long rein and tell him to turn it on. Most of them can't buck hard enough to scatter salt, but it feels good."

"I know what you mean," Hank said nodding. "When I fit a real good ride, I get a lot of satisfaction out of it. I think, 'Hell, I can go on doing this forever,' but then I have to get out the liniment in the morning."

As Sam turned the pickup east on Main Street, the

traffic light at the next intersection turned red. While he waited for the light to change, a girl with long legs encased in skintight Levi's crossed the street in front of the pickup.

"Lord, look at that, will you," Hank said fervently.

When the girl reached his side of the truck, Hank leaned out the window and called out, "You sure are pretty. Are you friendly?" After glancing at him, the girl turned away and walked gracefully along the sidewalk swinging her arms in rhythm with her bulging rump.

"Look at the motor on her," Hank said. "Enough to take a man's mind off his business." Sam smiled, but he was uncomfortable.

The light changed, and Sam put the pickup in gear.

"Can't you think of something you need at the five and dime store where that pretty girl turned in?" Hank asked. "I'd be happy to run an errand for you."

"Can't think of a thing I need," Sam said, "but I do have to mail this letter for Lucy before I forget."

He parked the truck next to a mailbox and got out, after taking a blue envelope from behind the sun visor. Sam glanced at the address on the letter. It was going to Jane Enright, Lucy's roommate when she went to college. Sam remembered her as a tall slender woman with very long, very straight blond hair that she was always tossing over her shoulders so it would fall down her back. She had been Jane Enright Marshall when she and her husband had visited them for a weekend three years ago. The husband had impressed Sam as being an irritating sort who asked lots of questions that were none of his business. He let Sam know that he made a great deal of money advising people in high tax brackets how to invest their money, and said that he was putting his client's "excess capital" into cattle. Sam did not follow all the details of the system, but it seemed that by means of some sort of limited partnership an investor could postpone payment of taxes for up to six years and claim immediate deductions on current taxes. For every $10,000 invested you could deduct $15,000 from your current tax bill, Marshall said. Sam did not understand how that could be, but he accepted it as another aspect of high finance he was destined not to comprehend. Everyone seemed able to get rich off cattle except him. Marshall went on and on about capital gains and something that sounded like a "double declining balance method of depreciation."

While Lucy and Jane tried to get caught up after so many years of sporadic correspondence, Sam had shown Roy Marshall around the Rocking R and found that he was unable to answer most of the broker's questions. Marshall had heard of Spencer Butterfield and evinced great curiosity about the finances of the ranch.

"I can't tell you much about the outfit in terms of dollars and cents," Sam said. "I don't sell much of the stock. Most of it goes to the California operations. They pasture them or feed them out to kill. I can tell you about how the calf crop percentage has risen right along with the weaning weight, or how much we can put on a *corriente* steer shipped up from the Magdalena Ranch and pastured here over the summer. I can give you the figures on how many heifers we breed as long yearlings to calve the next April so they'll get into the cow herd sooner than if we waited and bred them as twos. I can't tell you anything about our profit, but I know that we're very careful to keep the number of cattle on the ranch down according to the kind of year we've had for grass. We always try to make sure that there is more feed than we have to have, and that the range gets a chance to rest and recover. The only thing we add to the natural feed is salt. We pack salt blocks all over to keep the cattle spread out, using all of the range. Since we don't spend any money on expensive supplements, we can raise beef cheaper than most outfits. I can send the California operations calves and yearlings for a lot less than the going market price. That was what Butterfield had in mind when he put this spread together, and it seems to have worked out."

Sam hefted the letter. It was heavy, but he saw that Lucy had put double postage on the envelope. She must have had a lot to say, he thought. Funny, the way we are so different. Except for those notes I wrote home during the war, I have never been much of a letter writer, or any other kind of a writer for that matter. Thank God Spencer Butterfield and I do our business by phone. When did I write a letter last, anyway? Can't recall. And Lucy writes so much—letters, poems, whatever—and always has. I can't think of anybody else who likes to write. Everybody I know likes to spin yarns, but they would never think to write them down. I've heard some of the yarns time and time again, and no matter who tells them, they always say it happened to them. It makes the story better, and what the hell, it might just as well have happened to them. Old Floyd and his hitchhiker who points a gun at him and tells him to take a drink—I've heard that tale over and over from Montana to Mexico, and everybody who ever told it swears it happened to them. Floyd and the rest like to get together and swap stories, but Lucy would rather get off by herself and write them down. Well, bless her heart, whatever she wants to do suits me.

He pushed the fat letter into the mouth of the mailbox with only a moment's curiosity about what Lucy had written to her friend.

3

AS A CHILD Lucy had been drilled in handwriting by her mother, who was a former schoolteacher, and the result was a graceful, flowing script in which she took pride. The letter that Sam mailed was a model of the Palmer method of writing: slightly slanted, precise, and clear. The lines of black ink on the blue paper said:

Dear Jane:

Your long letter was so welcome, but it was such a mixture of glad and sad news. Your new home sounds marvelous and I know that you will have a grand time decorating it. (You have always been much more clever at that sort of thing than I.) I know that the separation and divorce were hard on you and the children, but now that is all behind you and you can start a new life.

Something you said in your letter bothered me. You said that you feel sorry for me "being stuck out in the wilderness." You must have really meant that you would feel sorry for yourself if you had to live out here, because you should know that there is no place I would rather live. Of course I don't have access to the company and entertainments you thrive on, but I neither need nor want them. When Sam and I were married fourteen years ago he worried a lot about how I would get along out on the ranch. He knew how hard the place had been on his mother, how lonely and isolated she had felt, and he didn't want me to suffer the ordeals that she had. What he didn't understand was that I could not wait to get out here. I was terribly unhappy in town. Baxter is such a stuffy place. Out here I have a fine feeling of freedom and of belonging.

You see, I look on the land as a community. The land, the livestock, the wild animals, the weather, the trees and grass and creeks, the sun and rain and snow, are all part of that community, and so am I. I love it and respect it and it nourishes me. I live a good life, in a much easier age than Sam's mother ever knew. She had no electricity or running water in the old house for most of the years she lived here. She had to cook for the crew, but I have help. She had to do laundry by hand and heat water on a wood stove. She worked from long before daylight in the morning until after dark at night. I have time to enjoy myself, to explore, to help Sam, to work on my poems. In a day's ride I can visit different climates from the tropical to the alpine. I can go from the floor of the desert to above the timberline on top of our mountain, Baldy. Up there are some little flowers that also grow above the Arctic Circle, and there are huge spruce and fir and pine trees at different altitudes. There are meadows up there of the brightest green you can imagine, all spangled at times with Indian paintbrush, lupine, poppies, lady's slipper, and wild geranium. At the edges of the meadows the white trunks of the aspens stand out against the dark evergreens. Deer browse in the bracken and shrubs, and squirrels with tufted ears scamper in the trees.

I know a dark pond up there. It is a natural basin in a sandstone formation. The sediment and silt have plugged the pores in the rock so thoroughly that the bowl holds runoff water the year around. If I sit very still beside this permanent pond, on a warm afternoon, I can watch quail families come to drink and dust themselves in the sand. A flight of blue-winged teal will zip in and splash down flashing their iridescent colors. This activity disturbs a big owl who has been sleeping in a tree beside the pond, causing it to ruffle up its feathers in a show of indignation. Mourning doves fly in on whistling wings and pace the rim of the pond. Above the soft notes of the doves I hear the harsh cry of the jays, and in the distance, out over the plains below, an eagle screams.

I can ride down from the mountain through juniper and piñon to the flats of sage and waving grass where I often see the white rumps of a band of tawny pronghorn antelope racing away. They usually stop on a rise and look back, their varnished black horns glinting in the sun. I know this herd. They range no farther than our cattle do, from this high plateau in the summer to the desert during the winter. Their kids are born in April and May, just when our cows are calving, but they have a shorter gestation period than the cows and don't breed until fall. Both sexes are horned, but the horns of the females are smaller than the males. After the breeding season they don't shed their horns, the way the buck deer drop their antlers, but the shiny black outer covering peels off and it takes a while for the new shell to harden. During that period they are very careful to avoid brush and trees because their horns are tender and sensitive. I love to watch them run, not just because they are one of the fastest animals on earth, but because they run so effortlessly. They sometimes seem to run for the pure joy of running, bounding and springing high with their slender wiry legs.

Below the plains lies the desert floor all speckled with greasewood, mesquite, and yucca. There are patches of scrub oak and now and then a palo verde with its bright green trunk and branches. The desert blossoms in the spring, with marvelously varied colors and splendid aromas. You may think of the desert as a lifeless place, but it is anything but barren. It teems with life. In addition to the birds, lizards, snakes, rabbits, mice, and other reptiles and rodents, there are my favorites: the coyotes. Coyotes are my favorites because they are so smart, and because they seem to laugh a lot. They trot along tirelessly, almost invisible in their earth-colored fur, and when they stop to look things over they grin a foxy grin as though they knew some secret joke. Of course, if we raised sheep, I would not feel so fondly toward them.

The Navajos call the coyote God's dog and credit him with infinite wisdom. After watching them over the years I can understand why. When I find where a pair of them have made their den I can spend days watching them with field glasses. There is one particular pair that I have become very attached to and I try to locate them every spring. I can identify the female because she has lost the tip of her left ear somehow, and because I got to know her at close range a few years ago. It was in the late winter, almost spring, and our male shepherd dog, Mick, disappeared for several days. Molly, the female dog, has been spayed because we did not want her to have pups, but Mick has not been altered and he, evidently, got wind of a female coyote in heat. I don't know how but he managed to pair up with her. You see, coyotes are usually monogamous and since the male plays a large role in raising the young the females are very selective when they decide to choose a mate. The pair runs together for a while before they breed. I guess this gives them a chance to get acquainted and see if they really want to bond to one another. Once they mate they stay together and the male hunts for the female while she is nursing the pups. Perhaps Mick found this little bitch in her first season. Anyway, they stayed together for a while and then, faithless domestic that he is, Mick got hungry and came home. He just didn't understand the responsibility he had assumed. Those instincts have been bred out of dogs.

Well, we were glad to see our Mick and made a fuss

over how thin he was. He lay around the house for a few days hardly able to move. One morning when Sam came back to the house after chores he told me that a coyote had been hanging around the edge of the woods beside the horse pasture. I got my field glasses and spotted her. I watched her for days and got to know her habits. She would come to the meadow each morning and sit looking toward the house with her one whole ear and the other cropped one pointed our way. She was a tiny thing and couldn't have weighed more than fifteen pounds. Her fur was more gray than brown. After sitting a long while she would begin to pace and then would vanish into the woods. In the evening she would appear again, sitting and staring at the house until dark while that rascal Mick snoozed on his rug in front of the fire. Then one morning she didn't turn up and I didn't see her again until years later, when I spotted her down on the desert hunting with a large male coyote. I found where they had their den and spent a lot of time studying them that spring. They had four puppies and I watched them grow. The adult pair would hunt together in the morning. If they found a prairie-dog village one would trot nonchalantly through the burrows sending the inhabitants underground while the other came stealthily along afterward. If one of the curious little ground squirrels poked its head up to see if the first coyote had gone away the second would grab it. As the pups got bigger the parents would take them out on hunts. At first the little ones spent most of their time roughhousing with one another, but gradually they began to practice pouncing the way their parents did. The adults would spot a mouse in a clump of grass and jump into the grass with their front feet. When the mouse moved they would snap it up and toss it in the air. The puppies scrambled for the mouse and it was not long before they were pouncing on clumps of grass themselves. They seldom produced a mouse, and when they did disturb one they couldn't catch it, but they were learning and having a fine time.

I have tried to keep track of my little crop-eared bitch and her big handsome mate. They seem like old friends now. I've always wondered whether or not she bore Mick's puppies. I know that dogs and coyotes can interbreed. They have the same number of chromosomes and it is genetically possible (remember Biology II?), but whether those offspring would be programmed to the breeding cycle of the full-blooded coyotes, I don't know. That is, if Mick's half-coyote pups survived, would they behave like coyotes and only breed once a year in late winter, or would they inherit the domesticated dog's year-round heat cycle? I'll have to look that up. In any event, I have not seen any coyotes that look in the least like Mick, and I really hope I don't. You know he and Molly were born with bobbed tails. If that is a dominant gene, and could possibly prevail in crossbreeding, I think it would be awful to see a short-tailed coyote. Would those puppies have the bonding instincts of coyotes, or would they behave like dogs?

What a mess we make when we upset the natural order of things!

We have tried to interfere with nature as little as possible. We have built no new roads and have kept the fencing to a minimum. The cattle live in harmony with the land and the seasons, just as the deer and antelope and elk do. Yes, we have a herd of elk in the high country. There are no more wolves or grizzly bears, but we have mountain lions and black bears up on Baldy. There are no more wild horses on the ranch, but we have horses by the hundreds, and you know how I love horses. I don't think I ever told you how foolish I was about horses when I was a child. Living right in the middle of town as we did I could not own a horse, but my room was filled with figurines and pictures of them. For a long time I pretended that I had an imaginary horse. I even made a stall for it in our woodshed and kept hay and straw in the stall. In the afternoon when school was over I would hurry home and pretend to clean out the stall, fluffing up the straw bedding. I talked to my horse and would have slept there if my father had let me. I think I really believed that some day my fantasy horse would materialize in that stall. Of course it never did, but now I have all kinds of horses: young ones to train, trained ones who make work a pleasure, a herd of dowager brood mares and dainty fillies, some magnificent sexy stallions, weanling, yearling and two-year-old colts, and the fuzzy-tailed infants running with their mothers. A paradise of horses!

Sam has taught me so much about them that I feel quite expert. He is just fantastic handling horses. It still thrills me to see him ride, even though sometimes

I think he takes too many chances. He has slowed down a little, but not much. He still seems to look at physical risks as opportunities, where I see them as dangers. But when he is well mounted and going flat out, he is something to behold. He likes to tease me and say that his idea of a good time is "to chase the wild bovine through the thick brush down the steep mountainside, going so fast it makes my eyes water." I love to ride out and work with him, but the above is not my idea of fun. I take pleasure in a strong, well-trained horse who has a free-swinging walk and an easy lope. My favorite ride is right after the first heavy snow, when the world is all clean and white and the fence posts have mushroom caps of snow on top. The land is so smooth and soft and silent. Later, delicate little footprints will appear everywhere, but on that first ride the snow is like white satin and it softens every contour. On such a ride I envy no one.

So please don't think of me as being "stuck" out here. Nothing on earth could be more to my liking.

Forgive me for going on so about the ranch. It is just that when I was a girl my mind was such a grab bag of desires that I didn't really know what I wanted, and now I feel fulfilled.

Please write when you find the time. I do enjoy your letters.

Love,
Lucy

Two black and gray Australian shepherd dogs greeted the pickup enthusiastically as Sam drove into the yard at headquarters followed by Hank in his car. Sam got out and spoke to the dogs.

"This is home," he told Hank, nodding toward the house with a long veranda. "That," he said, pointing to a solid-looking log house up the sloping ground to their right, "is where we lived when I was growing up. Spencer Butterfield built us this new house when Lucy and I got married."

The screen door to the new house opened and a woman with a compact figure and dark curly hair stepped out onto the porch. She was wearing Levi's and a blue chambray shirt faded from many washings. Sam smiled and waved to her.

"There's my lady," he said. "Let's see if she'll let us have something to eat."

"Godamighty," Hank said softly, "you told me she was smart, but you didn't say a thing about beautiful."

Supper was over and the dishes were done. The big ranch-house kitchen was cool as dusk descended. They sat relaxed around the kitchen table.

"I'm going to feed the dogs," Lucy said, and went outside with a covered pot in her hand. Sam watched her go across the porch and heard the shepherds whine as she talked to them.

"I'm going to have to get an early start in the morning," he said. "You just get up when you feel like it. When I get back I'll show you around."

"I'll roll out early if you want some help," Hank said.

"No need. I've just got to get up to our summer

range and tell the men there about the gather. After lunch you can help us move some horses down from pasture."

Hank stretched his long legs and slouched in the straight-backed wooden chair. He nodded his long face toward the screen door saying, "I guess you know that's a dandy lady you picked yourself."

Sam smiled and shook his head, "You're right and you're wrong. She's finer than dandy, but I can't claim any credit for picking her. I was gun-shy of marriage. Always figured if I wanted to do something dumb I should be the only one to regret it. Just me—not me *and* a wife. Lucy came along and said she wanted to do anything I wanted to do, dumb or not."

"Well, she's a winner," Hank said. "I got married twice and made a mess of it both times. I guess wives and rodeos just don't mix. What's it like living with a smart one? The women I meet are all sort of short in the smart department."

"She's way ahead of me," Sam said. "No question about it."

There were footsteps on the porch and Lucy came in. They both smiled at her as she joined them at the table.

"Molly has something the matter with the left side of her mouth, Sam," she said in her husky voice that did not seem to match her slender figure. "She keeps tipping her head to the right to chew."

"I know," Sam said, drawing his lips thin and nodding. "She went after another porky the other day. I thought I got all the quills out, but there must still be one under her gum. That's the damndest dog you ever saw, Hank. Smart as they come. Works stock like a genius. But she can't leave porkypines alone. I was scouting around horseback the other day and she and Mick were with me. Rode by the edge of a stand of pine trees and I heard Molly begin to whine. When I looked back both dogs had stopped and were looking into the woods. I stopped and sat my horse and watched. Mick went to the edge of the clearing and sort of sniffed toward the woods. He gave his head a shake and trotted on up to where I was. Old Molly, she sat there, whining as much as to say, 'I know I'm going to regret it, but I've got to run that prickly bastard off.' She whined and shook her head and wiped her muzzle on her front leg like she was already feeling those quills in her mouth. I called her and told her to leave the damn thing alone. She whined and dove into the woods. Mick and I watched. Pretty quick we heard her yelp, and then here she came sniffing and shaking her head and pawing at her muzzle. She trotted up and looked at me with her eyes all sad and gray quills sticking out of her nose and lips like whiskers. I got down and took my fence tool and went to pulling quills. They're tough to get out and hurt like hell.

"I sat down and Molly crawled onto my lap and let me work on her while she whined and sniffed. I had to take my shirt off and put it in her mouth when I went to get the ones inside. The shirt kept her mouth open and I could reach in and grab the pesky quills with the fence pliers. She just lay there like she knew she had to take her punishment. When I thought I had got them all out, I turned her loose and put my shirt back on. Molly ran over and licked Mick and they frisked around like they were both glad that was over.

"I don't know what it is about porkies. Molly is so damned intelligent about everything else. She studies your face to see what kind of mood you're in, and I swear she understands everything we say. She really thinks. But get her near a porkypine and she loses all her sense. She knows she's going to regret it, but she just can't leave them alone."

Hank chuckled and said, "Reminds me of some humans I know. They know something isn't good for them, but they go after it anyway."

"Molly is about half human," Sam said.

"What puzzles me," Lucy said, leaning her elbows on the table, "is that Molly is so much smarter than Mick in almost every other way, yet Mick ignores porkies because he knows he can't win that fight. He'll chase a rabbit or a ground squirrel, but when a porky comes along he looks the other way."

"As far as I know," Sam said, "Molly's never killed one. She ought to know better. Oh, well, I guess she'll never learn. Hon, you want to help us move some horses tomorrow?"

"Of course," Lucy said quickly with a smile, "you know I do. What time?"

"Afternoon. In the morning I've got to go up and tell Jake about the steer roundup. Right now I've got to call the boss and tell him about those Rocking R yearlings in Pima County. Pray for me."

Sam left the kitchen and went into the small room at the back of the house which he used as his office.

"He really dreads making this call," Lucy said. "Spencer Butterfield is definitely not going to like hearing what Sam has to tell him."

"I guess not," Hank said. "Have you had this kind of trouble before?"

"No," Lucy said. "Not here, but recently we've heard all kinds of stories about cattle being stolen in other parts of the state. Whole truckloads at a time."

She ran a hand through her short dark hair and rose in response to a scratching at the screen door. When she opened it, the two Australian shepherds scrambled in, skidding on the linoleum. The dogs were medium-sized, and their fur was multicolored splotches of black and gray that merged in places to a shade of blue. They had wide heads with short muzzles and dark, intelligent eyes. After sniffing the hand that Hank held down to them, they went to the two oval rag rugs by the window and lay down.

"Fine-looking dogs," Hank said. "They must be good company for you."

"Yes," Lucy said, smiling as the dogs stared up at her, wagging their stubby tails. "They're good company, and lots of help working stock."

"Is it lonesome for you way out here?" Hank asked gently.

"Not really. There are always people around, and lots to keep me busy. Right now most of the crew are scattered around in line camps, but there are a few here. A Navajo girl cooks for them. Pauline Begay.

She and I are good friends. I'm teaching her to play the piano and she's teaching me Indian poems. I write a little poetry, just for myself, and these Indian songs and verses are fascinating. I help Sam a lot because I'd rather be horseback and out with him than in the house. No, I don't get lonely. I don't have time."

"Yeah," Hank said, "I guess there's plenty of work involved in running an outfit this size. It's sure good to see old Sam again. You know, he was one helluva bronc rider."

"Yes," Lucy said. "He was good even before he went on the circuit. I used to watch him in our little rodeos when I was still in pigtails. I went to all the rodeos he rode in and all the high school football games he played in. He never knew I was there, of course. I was just a child, and he was the high school hero. Then he went off to the war and when he came back he joined the RCA and took off."

"That's when I met him," Hank said. "Spring of forty-six. We hit it right off and traveled together for almost three years. He got better and better, and then he up and quit. Said it wasn't fun anymore. I couldn't figure it out. He just packed it in right after Pendleton in the fall of forty-eight."

"Boy, is he ever steamed," Sam said, coming back into the kitchen. "He's really on the prod. I finally got him down at the Magdalena Ranch in Sonora. He'll be up here as soon as he can, and that means I've got to come up with some answers fast."

"Can I help?" Hank asked.

"You bet you can," Sam said. "I told you I was going

to make you earn your keep. Before we're through, bull riding is going to seem like a vacation."

As they were getting ready for bed, Lucy said, "Sam, how in the world do you suppose some one managed to steal those steers?"

"Beats the hell out of me," Sam said. "I'm going to get Jake and Martin to check out the river fence; and then we'll gather the steers and count them. Tell Pauline some extra men will be here for supper Saturday."

"I feel almost as though I'd been raped," Lucy said quietly, and took Sam's hands in hers. "Promise me you'll be careful. I mean if you come across anybody out there."

"They're long gone," Sam said. "Don't worry."

He sat down on the edge of the bed and pulled his scarred boots off and stared at them.

"I just wish I knew what I'm up against," he said quietly. "I don't even know what to look for. When you stop and think about it, it just doesn't seem possible. I mean, north of us is nothing but badlands, on the west is the river, and to the east it's either real rough country like Cottonwood Canyon or malpais lava breaks. The only way in to where the steers are is the road right here at headquarters. What it comes down to is that there's no way anybody could get any stock out of here without help from the inside. Somebody that knew their way around would have to set it up."

"I just can't believe that," Lucy said.

"I don't want to either," Sam said, "but that's how it looks."

"But we know it couldn't be Martin Yazzi or Jake Scott," Lucy said. "It just couldn't be them, and they're the only ones up there."

Sam shook his head and stared at his battered boots. "It doesn't seem possible," he said, "but how else can you explain it?"

"What does Red think?"

Sam ran a hand through his sand-colored hair. "Oh, he's all hot to get up here with airplanes and helicopters. I told him we'd handle this Butterfield's way: horseback. I'm caught in the middle between Butterfield and Red. You know how they're both used to having things their way."

"Well," Lucy said, kissing Sam on the cheek, "just promise me that you won't take any chances."

"It's funny," Sam said, "but I was thinking about that this morning, before I knew about this rustling business. I was thinking that things were getting kind of dull."

When they were in bed and the light was out, Lucy said, "Sam, I know he is an old friend of yours, but do you think there could be any connection between the stolen steers and Hank just showing up after all these years?"

"Oh, hell no," Sam said.

"I know it seems silly," Lucy said, "but there's something about him that makes me uneasy. He's just as nice as he can be, but he makes me feel edgy."

"Hank's all right," Sam said. "He just can't figure out what he's going to do when he has to quit rodeoing."

4

EARLY THE NEXT MORNING Sam left headquarters in the battered blue pickup and drove along the rough road that led up toward the northeast. Gradually the cedar and piñon pine gave way to jack pine, and then towering ponderosa, which were interrupted by patches of green meadows. When he broke out on top of the long climb a vast tableland of golden grama grass stretched away in front of him for miles to the broken rimrock on the horizon ahead. A bald mountain peak jutted up in the west. The road was smoother here, and Sam relaxed his grip on the steering wheel as he studied the grass. This was the summer range, where eight thousand mother cows and their calves grazed. At over six thousand feet, this range was too high for cattle in the winter, so when the first frost came, they would begin to drift south to the lower prairie of bunch grass and alfilaria. When winter set in, the cows would move before the wind and find protection in the draws and breaks of piñon and juniper. On the desert floor they would browse until spring. By carefully controlling the number of cattle on the range and by giving the native grasses plenty of time to regenerate, a natural balance could be maintained, and the cattle would always be able to find feed. Without drift fences to pile up against in blizzards, the cows could shift for themselves. Without expensive supplemental feed to hold them on a part of the range where there was not enough natural feed, they rustled a living from the land. Any cow that showed signs of not being able to support herself was quickly culled from the herd so that only heifers born to cows who got out and found feed were turned into the herd as replacements.

"I want stretchers," Spencer Butterfield maintained. "I want long, big-boned cattle with a frame to grow meat on. None of those short, chunky, dumpling types. Our cattle are never going to any stock shows; they're going to be fed out and hung on a hook."

By keeping operating costs at a minimum, and avoiding many modernizations which most ranchers had come to accept as necessities, the Rocking R consistently produced calves and yearlings at considerably less expense than the modernized ranches could. It had not always been easy. There had been droughts, when the foundation herd had to be drastically reduced, and blizzards that had caused heavy death losses. But Spencer Butterfield's theories had worked in practice, and by keeping the land as natural as possible, by never overburdening it, by allowing the cattle freedom to live an almost feral life, the ranch had prospered. Every mother cow in the herd had been born on the ranch. From the freshest two-year-old heifer with her first calf, to the wide-mouthed ten-year-old cow with ridges of rings on her horns, each one was biologically in tune with the cycle of the seasons and the rhythm of the year. The Rocking R was their world, and they were familiar with all its aspects. Sam knew the Spanish name for their relationship to the range: *querencia.* When he was ten a Mexican cowboy who had ridden for the outfit had explained the word to him: "It is the land and sky, the grass and water, in the blood and breath of the cow. It lives in her and she lives in it and she is content. It is her place and part of her."

This is my *querencia* too, Sam was thinking as he drove across the tableland of grass. I've been out and around in the world, but nothing suits me the way this does. I just wish I could look forward to something besides payday. At that, I'm a lot better off than Hank. I've got Lucy, and I know who I am. I wonder why I'm uncomfortable with him now. He's exactly the same as he was sixteen years ago. Maybe that's the trouble. I've changed and he hasn't.

Sam scanned the mountain peak to the west. It would be cool up there at nine thousand feet. He envisioned a network of sparkling torrents tumbling down through the rocks, and into the shade of the big timber, haphazardly meandering until they came together to form the creeks that watered this plain. The bare peak glistened in the sun.

If you can find it on a map (and it is not on many) it will be referred to as Bald Mountain. The Indians knew it by several names, according to their tribe, and while they did not revere it as they did the peaks of the taller San Francisco Mountains to the east, which were their Olympus, they did give it a place in their legends. The early trappers saw its gleaming dome and dubbed it Baldy. So it is called today, by everyone except cartographers, who must differentiate between it and a taller peak far to the east called Mount Baldy.

From where it rises north of headquarters, Baldy dominates every vista on the Rocking R range. On most days it can be seen from as far as a hundred miles away, but at times its treeless top is shrouded in clouds. When it is not hidden in mist the peak changes colors as the sun strikes it from different angles during the day. Sometimes, in the very early morning, the lower slopes are hidden by haze and only the barren peak is visible, seeming to hang in the sky without support. But no matter where you are on the ranch, look up from what you are doing and you will see Baldy. You will know where you are and which direction you are heading by where the mountain is.

People will tell you that there is a lost silver mine somewhere on the mountain. There may be, but it has been lost for a very long time, and a great many people searched for it until Spencer Butterfield bought the land surrounding the mountain and let it be known that prospectors were not welcome. The story goes that in the 1870's one Jack Pascoe, a Cornish hard-rock miner turned prospector, learned from a hired Indian guide of a "mountain of silver" north of where they were camped. Pascoe wasted no time and was very soon outfitted with extra burros and supplies for the long trek north. He and the Indian moved as one must when traveling with burros: very deliberately. When he first set eyes on the mountain its dome of bare rock did indeed glisten like silver and Jack Pascoe pressed toward it with great excitement. But burros will not be hurried and for days the gleaming mountain seemed to get no closer. When, at last, they reached the base of the mountain and started to struggle up the steep slope, Pascoe began hacking out samples of rock as he climbed. He found no silver, not even any promise of it, and when he reached the tree line he found only a granite mass above. Furious, he turned on his guide. The Indian explained that the silver was beneath the dome of rock, and showed him where to dig.

They say that Jack Pascoe found a thick vein of almost pure silver and took out as much as his burros could carry. Then he killed the Indian and sealed the mouth of the mine with boulders cemented together by means of pulverized rock mixed with his hapless guide's blood. He planted brush across the walled-up entrance and obliterated all signs of his presence except for a cross which he chiseled into a huge flat rock above the mine. Then, so the story goes, he left and in time made his way to San Francisco, where he set sail for Cornwall. Years later he returned, evidently bent upon reopening the mine, but rockslides had so changed the face of the mountain that he was never able to relocate the mine entrance or to find any trace of silver. He stayed on the mountain for months, digging furiously, but was finally driven out by winter.

He ended his days as a mole in the copper mines at Globe, Arizona, but not before he had sold several copies of a map to the mine in the "mountain of silver." Well into the twentieth century, hopefuls equipped with not much more than copies of the copies of Jack Pascoe's maps struggled up the sides of Baldy, but no one has ever turned up any silver. If it was ever there it still is.

But beyond white men's myth and Indian legend, Baldy is a presence, all day, every day, aloof and serene. There are no roads on the mountain, but there is a game trail that leads to a high bench just below the tree line. Sam Howard rode up that trail and scattered his father's ashes from a rocky ledge in May of 1950. He offered no prayer, but he scanned the distance stretching out below and confirmed his slightly reluctant promise given to Spencer Butterfield: to take his father's place and run the Rocking R. He was not at all sure that he would be satisfied with measuring out his life to the seasonal cycle of ranch routine. But he had given his word, so that was that. Fourteen years later he was still not sure, but he had not gone back on his promise. From time to time he looked up at Baldy and reminded himself of his responsibilities and his rewards. Wherever he was he could always see the mountain.

Near the rocky ledge from where Sam had let loose the handful of smoke that had been his father, there is a fissure in the face of the mountain, a deep cleft in which animals have denned and man has never been. Now, in August of 1964, it is the home of a large male mountain lion. What you call him will depend on where you are from: puma, painter, panther, cougar, catamount, or whatever. In Arizona he is called lion, and those who know him respect him. That is as it should be, for he can break a horse's neck with one blow, overtake a startled deer in three twenty-foot leaps, and prevail over any adversary except a gun. This big cat eats deer, relishes horseflesh, and is at times reduced to a diet of rodents. He weighs almost two hundred pounds and his tawny body is six feet long with a yard more of tail added. He only weighed a pound at birth, but now he is six years old and in his prime. Unless he makes a mistake, he will live to be ten or fifteen. Up on Baldy he has nothing to fear. Sam Howard knows he is there because he has seen the extra-large tracks on the mountain trails, but Sam knows that the big cat belongs on the mountain the way the grass belongs on the high prairie. When Sam hears a female lion scream in the night, he likes to think that the big male has heard her announcing her readiness to breed. Sam likes to think of him padding softly through the dark, testing the air, solitary, but seeking out the scent which that scream has signaled from afar. Sam likes to look up at Baldy and picture the big cat sunning himself on a rock near the timberline, or stalking a deer, or watching Sam ride by below.

Baldy would not be the same without the presence of the big cat.

The road bent gradually toward the north, and as it did so, the horizon ahead of Sam became more and more irregular. In the distance jagged mesas hundreds of feet high and hogbacks with steep sides were silhouetted against the blank blue sky. The grassland ended as abruptly as it had begun, and at its edge, surrounded by stately pines that swayed together at their tops, was a sturdy set of corrals and a squat cabin made of peeled logs. Smoke wisped up from the cabin chimney as Sam drove into the yard. He stopped the truck and called out, "Anybody home?"

Without thinking about why he did so, Sam waited in the cab of the truck until a slim figure appeared in the doorway and shouted, "Hell, yes. Get down and come in." Only then did he open the door of the pickup and step to the ground. At another line camp he might simply have driven in and gotten out of the truck, but this was Jake Scott's camp, and at Jake's camp traditions were observed. Sam knew that in Jake's world you always hail a house before you get too close to it so as not to take anyone by surprise. Ritual requires that you remain mounted until invited to dismount, and if you are not invited, you are given to understand that you should move on without being told. When you do dismount you make sure that you are getting off toward the person greeting you so you are in full view all the time. This is as fundamental as greeting someone with an upraised empty hand, which says that you come in peace. Jake's ways were the old ways, and Sam had been brought up to respect them. He observed the conventions because it would be bad manners not to and it was important to show that he had been raised in the traditions of the West, that he played by the rules. He held Jake, and what he stood for, in great respect.

Old Jake came toward him walking a little pigeon-toed in a stiff-legged, rolling gait. He carried his elbows bent, and his knobby wrists thrust out from the frayed cuffs of a worn denim jacket. Sam watched him with affection and admiration; the old man had been a hero of his boyhood. From time to time, over the years, Jake had left the Rocking R to work in other parts of the West, but whenever he returned, there was always a place for him—a camp to take over, horses to train—and use for all the skills he had spent his life developing (they were not in much demand on the modernized ranches). The old man knew the Rocking R better than anyone else, and Sam needed his help now more than ever before.

"Morning, Jake," Sam said. "Coffee hot?"

"You bet," the old cowboy answered, accenting the first word, and rearranged the deep lines in his hickory brown face as he smiled a welcome.

They entered the cabin, and Sam glanced around the one-room structure. He had spent several of his boyhood summers here helping Jake, and the place had changed very little. The room was thirty by twelve feet with two metal-framed beds at one end and a black cast-iron wood stove at the other. Bridles, ropes and other pieces of gear hung from the walls on randomly placed pegs and nails. There were two windows in each of the longer walls, and none at the ends. A sturdy wooden table stood against the back wall, opposite the door, with three hide-bottomed chairs around it. The table was covered with red oilcloth and had a shiny new Coleman lamp on it. That was a change. Before, Sam remembered, the lamps had been kerosene. The sink was just the same, with its short-handled pitcher pump and chipped enamel. There were six other cabins strategically scattered around the ranch, some of them larger and better equipped than this one, but this was Jake's favorite. The old cowboy knew this range the way a gardener knows his own little plot of ground. He could sense when the different grasses attained their greatest strength, and he understood why the cattle kept some areas grazed down while other grass grew rank. He knew, but could not explain scientifically, why green grass produced milk for the nursing cows and then changed in its chemical composition, as it matured and dried, to produce bone and muscle. He understood that after the first hard frost the grama grass would fill the cows up, but nourish them very little, so they would gradually wean their calves and go dry, storing what energy they could for the unborn calves developing inside them. Jake Scott savvied the cow. He knew what a cow was going to do before the cow did, and he could tell from a great distance when something was the matter with one of them. He rode his country and husbanded his stock. He held to the old ways because they worked, and because of what they stood for.

Sam remembered one fall, when he was eleven. An early storm caught some Mexican steers in the high country and they had to be found before the snow became too deep for them to get down to the shelter of the canyons and breaks. Sam's father had taken several men in one direction and had sent Jake with two other hands and young Sam in another. They were to work their way up around where the cattle were seeking shelter, unwilling to move against the wind, and drive them down to where they could find feed on flats blown clear of snow. It was bitter cold. Sam had on so many clothes that he could hardly mount Blucher, but he was not far from the corrals before his feet began to go numb. Despite the scarves and sweaters, the gloves inside mittens, the chaps over two pairs of Levi's, and a blanket-lined jacket, the cold penetrated every part of his body. By the time they had climbed to where the cattle were Sam was miserable. He was determined not to complain or reveal in any way that the job was too much for him. He let Blucher wallow ahead on his own. He was only dimly aware of the frequent times that Jake and his frosty horse loomed out of the whiteness checking on him. The cattle resented being driven into the wind, and turned aside at every opportunity. Jake and the others whistled and cursed. Sam clung to his saddle horn with strengthless fingers as Blucher lunged into the drifts. The snow was blowing horizontally, and every breath burned. Long after Sam was sure that his hands and feet were frozen, Jake appeared out of the blinding whiteness and led the way down into a creek bed where they were sheltered from the wind. The steers moved more readily, and Jake dropped back to ride beside Sam.

"I tell you, Scout," Jake drawled through his muffler, "this work is losing its romance."

And here he is, Sam thought, old Jake; sixty, if he's a day, still tending his cows and gentling colts, living up to what he expects of himself. If that's good enough for him, why isn't it good enough for me?

"You must of got up before breakfast to be way up here by now," Jake said, pouring two mugs of dark coffee from a chipped, gray-enamel pot.

"Yeah," Sam said, taking one mug and blowing across its steaming rim. "We've got a problem. Red Farnsworth says fifteen head of yearling steers with badly worked-over Rocking R brands turned up in an auction yard down in Pima County the other day."

"The hell you say," Jake drawled, frowning.

Sam nodded. "We're going to have to tally the steers and find out if that was all that were stolen and just how in hell they got stolen."

"Sonofabitch," Jake muttered, scowling at the red oilcloth. "How could anybody get cattle out of that Bill Williams country without us knowing it? Don't seem possible."

"I know, Jake," Sam said, "but it looks like they did. You haven't cut any sign over here?" Jake shook his head. "Has the kid mentioned seeing anything?" Jake shook his head again.

"No," Jake said. "Past few weeks, when he wasn't packing salt with me, he's been working on the fence up north where the badlands start. A mountain goat couldn't get through that way. Besides, he couldn't track a elephant in three feet of snow."

They sipped the hot coffee. Jake squinted toward the open door and shook his head.

"Just don't seem possible," he drawled. "Spencer's gonna throw a fit."

"Not going to," Sam said, "*has!* I called him last night. He's down at Magdalena. The connection wasn't so good, but he got the message and came back loud and clear. You know *him.* He'll be up here shortly."

"Means we've got to gather the whole Bill Williams country," Jake said. "There ain't a cross fence in there anywhere."

"Yup," Sam said. "I've got some help coming out Saturday. This afternoon why don't you and Wild William move on over to Martin's camp. See if Martin has noticed anything and take a look around. Maybe they came in from across the river somewhere. I'll bring a crew up there Sunday, with the roundup wagon and remuda."

"Yeah," Jake nodded agreement. "It wouldn't hurt to prowl around some before the others get there and muss up any sign that might be there. Martin's sharp. If somebody came and went across the river, there's only a few places they could've made it, and they'd have to leave tracks. Me and him'll pick 'em up. Does Martin know about this?"

"No," Sam said, "I came straight here. I'll drive over there now. I brought you a couple of boxes of shells for the thirty-thirty, just in case. I didn't bring a gun for Will. Do you think I should?"

"Great Godamighty, no," Jake said fervently. "That crazy damn gunsel kid is dangerous enough as it is.

Thinks he's some kind of desperado. Last thing you want to do is give him a gun. Wants to shoot everything. Tried to sneak my rifle out when he went to wrangle the horses. I sez, 'Where in hell you think you're going with that?' He sez, 'There's a pair of coyotes that watch me every morning when I ride out to bring in the horses. I aim to shoot 'em.' I took the rifle away from him, and told him that when the coyotes started bothering the stock he could go to bothering them. He's hell-bent to shoot things. Quick as he saw a band of antelope he wanted to knock over a couple. I told him they tasted like billy-goat meat. He didn't care, just wanted to shoot 'em. We got a quarter of good yearling beef in the meat safe and he wants to go after antelope. Told him the meat's rank, and so tough he wouldn't be able to get a fork into the gravy, but he didn't care."

Jake shook his head, as if in despair of ever understanding the youngster, and Sam grinned because he remembered when Jake had chastised him for his wild ways when he was a boy.

"You don't just naturally have to meet every goddamn thing head on," Jake would say after Sam had done something foolish. "You don't have to do everything the hard way. Stop and think for once." But Sam knew that Jake was proud of him and his contempt for danger, even when the results were disastrous. "Now you've done done it!" Jake would shout, when Sam's headlong tactics caused an accident. "Purely bound and determined to kill us both, ain't you." But Jake had gone to great pains to teach him all the cowboy crafts and skills, even though he pretended exasperation. Sam was sure that Jake was fond of Will.

Will Michaels was a strange boy in many ways, but Sam liked him. Boots Taylor had brought him to the ranch to help with the calf branding in June, and at first Sam had been uncomfortable around the youngster because of the way he stared so intently when Sam was speaking. Will's open expression had the look of slightly stunned innocence. His large blue eyes were set far apart under his furrowed brow. He always seemed to be concentrating, and slightly puzzled. Boots explained that Will had hitchhiked across country from West Virginia, determined to find the Wild West that he had seen in the movies and to learn to be a cowboy before he went to Vietnam.

"He don't know nothing," Boots said when he told Sam the boy's history, "but he's hell for stout. I put him to work at the filling station, and you just can't wear him down. We can use him flanking calves and such."

"He don't look to me like he's playing with a full deck," Jake said.

"Well," Sam said, "maybe it helps to be a little feebleminded if you're setting out to cowboy. If you had all fifty-two you couldn't stand it."

Will worked so hard during the calf branding that he was able to persuade Sam to keep him on over the summer. Sam sent him up to camp with Jake so he could pack the heavy blocks of salt to distant parts of the range, check and repair windmills, fix fence, and do other chores. Jake had protested that he not only did not need help, but did not want any.

"Got no more use for that gunsel kid up there than a hog has for a sidesaddle," was the way Jake put it, but Sam had persuaded him to use Will's considerable strength stretching wire and hauling salt. Jake still complained about how reckless the boy was, but Sam sensed that they were getting along. Once, Sam arrived at their camp to find Will chopping a huge supply of stove wood while Jake was out riding his country, "interviewing the cows," as Jake put it.

"Jake is sure good at explaining things," Will told Sam. "All kinds of things. Like this wood. When I first went at it I was fighting it all the way. He showed me how to let the saw do the work. And when it came to the splitting, I'd make hard work out of that too. He showed me how to aim. Not dead center the way I was, but out toward the edge. My old man, he knows things, but he never explained nothing, always said I was too dumb to understand. Not Jake. He says, 'Take this part of the rope and hold it so, if you want it to do like this, and when you want it to do the other, hold it so.' We brought in a cow and calf the other day and put them in the corrals 'cause the calf looked like it had a foxtail or something in its eye. Jake told me to separate them so we could doctor the calf. I went to trying to drive that calf and was having a helluva time. Jake came back with the medicine and watched me and said, 'Always drive cows away from calves, not the other way around.' I left the calf where it was and drove the cow into the next pen as easy as you please.

We doctored the calf and let the cow back in when we were done. You can really learn things from Jake. He knows and he can explain."

I know, Sam thought, how well I know.

"All right," Sam said as he rose and took his coffee mug to the sink and rinsed it under the stubby little pump. "As soon as he comes in you and Will pack your beds over to the Bill Williams camp and prowl around for sign. We'll be up late Sunday and start the gather the next day."

"How close a tally you aim to make?" Jake asked.

"I want to see every damn one of them," Sam said. "I want to put them through a gate."

Jake nodded, and crinkled his eyes into a squint. "Which gate?" he said. "Not many over there."

"Well," Sam said, "if we work from north to south we can bring them all down into the bull pasture. It's empty, and there's plenty of grass to hold them till we've got them all. We can count them coming back up through the bull pasture gate. That way we won't knock many pounds off them. Just graze them along down to the lower range, and count them back out. Tell Will I don't want any chousing or rodeoing. Tell him if I catch him with his rope down I'll whip him with it."

Jake stretched his wrinkles into a grin and pushed his hat back uncovering his pale forehead.

"He must of got himself in some kind of a storm with that rope yesterday," Jake said. "He was being mighty careful with his right hand this morning."

"I guess that's the only way he'll ever learn," Sam said. "Can he handle his horses yet?"

"Not Beaver," Jake said, smiling. "Every time he puts a leg over him Beaver homesteads him. I'll say this for the boy: he's got more nerve than a outhouse rat. Beaver turned him into a windmill three times in a row the other day, and Will kept getting back on. He ain't got any give-up in him. One of these days he's going to surprise hell out of old Beaver and stay with him."

Sam nodded; it seemed to him that Will Michaels was well on the way to winning Jake's approval.

"I had to laugh a while back," Jake said. "That Kelly horse ran away with him. Kelly is kind of cold-jawed when he gets hot; he may have got a touch of the weed sometime back. Anyhow, I guess Will was pretending he was some sort of pony express rider; he's always asking me if I was ever a pony express rider, or a stage driver, like I was a hundred years old; and Kelly just stuck his nose out and took off coming home. Went past the cabin like a dose of salts through a bookkeeper. When he got to the corral old Kelly put down all four. Made the squarest, hardest, ball-bustingest stop you ever did see. Will just kept on going, right out over that pony's head, and hit the ground so hard he bounced twice. I like to bust a gut laughing. Old Kelly squatted there blowing, and Will bouncing. Next day I showed him how to double a runaway."

Sam smiled, and Jake chuckled and shook his head, saying, "Crazy goddamn gunsel kid."

When Sam reached the pickup he paused and turned toward Jake. "How in hell do you suppose those steers were rustled?"

"Damn if I know," Jake said, "but we'll find out, Sam. For sure, we'll find out, and cure whoever done it of the habit."

5

SAM LEFT JAKE'S CAMP and drove west along the rutted dirt road that led to the Bill Williams range, which was used as a summer pasture for yearling steers. As he guided the pickup he shaped his plans for the roundup and thought about the most likely campsites for the crew. The air was so clear that it sparkled, and the light was intense. Baldy thrust its bare-rock peak up into the brilliant blue, and the distant western mountains were a purple smudge on the skyline. Despite the distress he felt over the stolen steers, Sam was moved by the beauty of the land. He passed a half-dozen cows grazing with their calves in a group and automatically checked their general appearance. The calves were getting big. He loved to watch them grow. In June, when they were branded, these calves had been spindly little things, and now they were thickening. All the cattle raised their heads as he drove by, and two of the calves scampered hightailed a few bounds away before they stopped and stared.

Sam was not aware of it, but his passage was being observed from a distance by an old mother cow who was grazing with her calf on a bench above the level of the road. She watched the blue pickup without much concern since it was heading away from her; she would have been more disturbed by a man on horseback. By this time in her life, she had learned what men on horseback would do. Twice a year they would come and drive the cows and calves together in noisy confusion. In the spring her calf would return to her at the end of the day smelling of fire, blood and medicine. In the fall the calf would not return. So this old cow is wary of men on horseback. In many ways she is as feral as the mule deer that migrate across this range. If you could get closer to her you would notice that instead of the blank white face and forehead, which most of the Rocking R cows have, she has a splotch of red across her muzzle and around her left eye. She has a brockle-face. This marking does not turn up often in Herefords because the white face is a dominant gene in the breed. If you crossbreed a Hereford with a solid black Aberdeen Angus you will get a black calf with a white face. Breed a Hereford to a Shorthorn and you will get a red-roan calf with a white face. When a brockle-face heifer turns up in a herd of Herefords she is usually not turned back into the breeding herd because the patches of red on her face are considered undesirable, but on the Rocking R conformity in color patterns is not paramount. The important consideration is how well a cow earns her own living and produces calves. The cow with the splotchy face will be left alone until she fails to conceive; then she will be shipped for slaughter and converted into cans of soup.

But this year she has a healthy calf beside her, and a developing fetus in her womb, even though she is showing signs of age. She looks thin and her waist is tucked up, but that is only because she has been feeding her calf well. She is really in good flesh. While it is true that she does not shed off her shaggy winter coat as early in the spring as she used to, she is still nimble and quick. Her mouth has widened as her lower front teeth have worn and spread, the white tuft at the end of her tail has lengthened, and the ridges of rings at the base of her horns all testify to her longevity. Her horns are formidable. They curve forward gracefully from above her tufted ears, and thrust ahead to sharp tips that are level with her white eyelashes. She looks out at the world from behind these weapons, ready to jab and parry, to thrust and ward. She will fight anything that she and her calf cannot evade, including you. She charges with her head up and her eyes open, shifting her weight from one front foot to the other so that no last-minute side step will save you, as it might from a bull. She relies on the sharp tips of her horns to do the damage, not the plate of her forehead. She can hook, jab, and throw combinations like a very well trained boxer. She has driven away hungry bears and prowling coyotes when they have come to investigate the odor of afterbirth, and her calf was too new to run.

She will not hesitate to charge a man on foot because his silhouette is bearlike, and she does her best to hide from a man on horseback because he has taken calves from her before.

She is tender and attentive toward her calf and identifies it from all others by smell. If they become separated each will automatically return to wherever they were the last time the calf sucked. Some cows, ones that are not so fiercely preoccupied with the well-being of their own calves, will tolerate an orphan who steals a little milk. Not the brockle-face cow. She kicks trespassers off her teats and drives them away. All of her milk is for her calf only. As her calf learns to depend more and more on grazing, and as the grass cures and reseeds itself, she gives less and less milk. By late fall she dries up entirely and converts all of her intake toward developing the new calf growing inside her. Nine months after she was bred the calf is ready to be born. The brockle-face cow finds a place apart, protected from the wind, and as her uterine contractions heighten, she lies down. The spasms of her abdominal muscles force the calf against her cervix and out along the birth canal. The fetal membranes break as the calf's forefeet emerge, and are followed by its head. When the calf is out, the cow stands up and quickly licks it off, memorizing its smell. She starts at the muzzle and licks away any mucus that may clog the calf's nostrils. Her rough tongue stimulates circulation as it cleans the calf's wet coat. She boosts the calf to its shaky legs and positions herself so it can nurse. After testing her hind leg the calf finally finds her teats and is rewarded with a hot gush of magical colostrum. This first milk has been stored in the cow's udder building strength, and for the next three or four days it will provide the calf with a variety of antibodies for immunity to diseases, and with high doses of vitamins and minerals, as well as gamma globulin and protein. For these first few days the brockle-face cow and her calf will remain apart from the other cattle and change their bed ground often for safety from carnivores. Until the calf is sure enough on its feet the cow will leave it hidden while she goes to graze, but she will not go far. She has an instinct for survival.

The brockle-face cow *is* a survivor. Her ancestors developed oversized and complicated stomachs, which enabled them to snatch great quantities of food in a hurry out in exposed meadows, and retreat to safer surroundings quickly, before a saber-toothed tiger caught them. Her stomach, fifty gallons in capacity, is a marvel of efficiency and can digest almost anything. In tall grass she wraps her long rough tongue around the tufts and draws them into her mouth between her eight front lower incisors and the tough horny pad above (cattle have no upper teeth in the front of their mouths). With a quick sideway snatch of her head she cuts the grass and swallows it without chewing it up. Well wetted down by her highly alkaline saliva, the grass is stored in the largest section of her commodious stomach, the rumen, where bacteria and protozoa ferment it and begin breaking it down into usable protein. What does not break down readily is regurgitated later and chewed between her twelve back molars. This pulp that is brought up for chewing is her cud. Anyone who husbands cattle likes to see them lying down early in the day, calmly ruminating, because that means that they have gotten full quickly and feed is plentiful. If they have to graze all day it is a sign that there is not enough feed to fill them up quickly. During warm weather cattle feed early so they can find shade to rest in and ruminate when the heat becomes intense. That is why cowboys get up early.

Early one spring morning, when men on horseback came whistling and popping the tails of their bridle reins against their leather chaps, the brockle-face cow led her calf deep into a thicket, and lay down facing her back trail. A cowboy rode by and peered into the brush, but the cow's mottled face camouflaged her, and the horseman passed on. She and her bull calf spent the summer unmolested in the roughest parts of the ranch, and when they were finally rounded up in the fall it was too late to castrate the bull calf and turn him into a steer. Since he was big and sturdy it was decided that he would be raised as a replacement bull. Between the heifers which the brockle-face cow has provided for the foundation herd, and the bull calf, which has come to be known to the men as Mussolini, the old cow's sturdy characteristics will be found in the Rocking R cattle for a long time to come.

When Sam got out to open the gate at the steer pasture fence he studied the ground for tracks, but found none. After closing the gate and wiring it shut he drove toward a speck in the distance, the windmill at the Bill Williams camp. He hoped that Martin Yazzi would not be out riding his country — he did not want to have to wait for him to come back — but he knew that hands were embarrassed to be found in camp: they did not want him to think they spent their time loafing. The land began to drop as it stretched away toward the river, and the color of the earth grew darker with every passing mile. As Sam drove into the yard in front of the low house of unpainted weathered planks he was glad to see the tall man in the corral rubbing down a sweaty colt. The cowboy acknowledged Sam's arrival with a glance and went back to stroking the colt with a folded feed sack. Sam got out of the pickup and walked to the corral. There he waited, leaning on the top pole. He could hear Martin murmuring as he rubbed the colt. Sam lit a Lucky Strike and inhaled, studying the young horse, which was standing quietly. Sam knew the colt; it was a three-year-old out of Dolly, a mare whose first foal had been a horse colt that had turned out to be one of Sam's favorites: Rebel. The colt that he had turned over to Martin was a full brother to Rebel, and Sam was interested in how it was coming along.

Sam had finished his cigarette when Martin turned the colt loose to roll in the corral dirt and joined him at the fence. Martin was a head taller than Sam, and much heavier. He wore a black hat and tied his black hair at the back of his head with several wraps of thick white cotton string. His face was broad, and his eyes sparkled like polished ebony. As Sam told him about the stolen steers Martin's expression tightened, and the wrinkles at the corners of his eyes grew deeper. He shook his head in disbelief.

"Sam, there's just no goddamn way anybody could get fifteen head of these steers out of here without my knowing it," he said with conviction.

"What about the river," Sam said. "It's low. Could they swim them across, say at the big gravel bar or down by Echo Canyon?"

"Not unless they knew how to walk on top of quicksand," the big Indian said, shaking his head. "I'll check out the river fence, but I've been all up and down there recently and didn't see anything but my own tracks."

"Jake and Will are on their way over here," Sam said. "They can help. I'll be up with a crew and remuda late Sunday and we'll count the steers. It might be a good idea for you and Jake to butcher a yearling between now and then."

Martin nodded and studied the western mountains.

"Sam," he said, "give me a gun."

"You think that's a good idea?" Sam said quietly.

Martin nodded. "If some sonofabitch is stealing our cattle, he's got a lesson coming to him."

They walked to the pickup where Sam took a lever-action Winchester down from the rack across the rear window of the cab and handed it to Martin. He opened the glove compartment and brought out a flat box of cartridges.

"For God's sake don't use it unless you have to," Sam said earnestly.

Martin held the short rifle in one powerful hand and

the ammunition in the other. He scowled and said softly, "Don't worry, I just feel better having it."

Sam studied the tall, broad-shouldered man and remembered something he had said a few years ago. Sam could not recall how the grizzly subject had come up, but he knew that he would never forget hearing Martin say, in a very matter of fact way, "Gas is what makes a corpse come to the surface. If you want to keep a dead man from floating, gut him and fill him with rocks. That way he'll stay down till the fish eat him." Sam remembered suppressing the urge to ask Martin how he knew this technique, which he had described as simply as if he were explaining how to mount a horse. He had never told anyone about it, not even Lucy, just as he had never told her about Martin's prison record. He and Red were the only people around Baxter who knew anything about Martin's past. That was as it should be, he thought.

"Well," Sam said, "I've got to go down below and run in the remuda. Do you want me to bring you up some extra horses Sunday?"

"Wouldn't hurt," Martin said. "We'll be working some big circles. I'll go pick out a yearling and pen him up here. Me and Jake can beef him when it gets cooler."

It was time for lunch when Sam drove into the yard at headquarters. Mick and Molly met him with their usual enthusiasm, and Lucy was excited at the prospect of gathering the big horse pasture.

"She dearly loves to run horses," Sam explained to Hank. "It's her favorite sport."

"You're right," Lucy said. "I'd sure rather do horse-work than housework."

"I'm looking forward to it myself," Hank said, "but you're going to have to tell me what to do."

"Nothing to it," Sam said. "These'll all be broke saddle horses, used to being brought in. They know there'll be some grain waiting for them. All we have to do is start them this way. If it was a band of brood mares, or old Barney's flock of fillies, we'd need help. The three of us can handle the geldings."

"Old Barney is a gray gelding who is so wind-broken he can't be worked anymore," Lucy explained, "so he runs with the fillies and they band up on him. You see, each spring we vaccinate all the yearlings and turn them out. The horse colts go to a big rough section of the ranch and learn to run in rocks. They don't get saddled till they're three. The fillies get put in a rough pasture too, with Barney, who adores them all. They stay out until they're two, and then we bring them in and cull them. We sell the culls and breed the keepers to whichever stallion we think will nick best. After their first foal has been weaned they join one of the bands of brood mares, and each band has its stallion. Barney is the eunuch stallion of the filly herd. He watches over them and is just as proud as if he were a stud."

"I think," Sam said, "Barney believes every first foal born on the ranch is his."

"He gets foolish, but he's a dear," Lucy said, smiling.

"Do you sell many horses?" Hank asked.

"Just the culls," Sam said. "The fillies that we don't

much like the looks of and the colts that aren't real promising when we break them. You can tell everything you need to know about what kind of horse he is going to turn out to be when you start working on a three-year-old colt."

"We've always wanted to enlarge the horse herd," Lucy said, "and raise them commercially, but we haven't been able to persuade Spencer Butterfield to let us."

"He needs cattle in California," Sam said, "not horses."

"Some day he'll give in," Lucy said. "You wait and see."

"I'm not going to hold my breath," Sam said.

On the long ride to Martin's line camp where the steers were pastured, Will Michaels kept up a steady stream of questions. They herded their extra horses along ahead and rode abreast at an easy jog. Jake studied the grass, the direction of the wind, and the clouds hanging above the far mountains. He rode a small buckskin horse that carried its head low, level with the saddle. Jake's legs were straight down his stirrup leathers, his weight balanced on the balls of his feet so that the spring in his knees would absorb the beat of the jog. Will sat on his saddle and jiggled away. Baldy glistened in the clear sky to the south on their left.

"If you get turned around over here and lose track of where you are," Jake said, nodding toward the mountain, "just check on where Baldy is. Try to keep track of where the sun is as you go along, and between the sun and the mountain you oughta be able to keep from getting lost. This time of year the wind is apt to be out of the northwest."

"What's that over there, Jake, a eagle?"

"Naw, turkey buzzard."

"Means something's dead?"

"Means he's *looking* for something dead."

"Could you hit him from here?"

"Why should I?"

"Could you?"

"Maybe."

"Try."

"No."

"Jake, who was the best all-round cowboy you ever knew?" Will asked, looking at him earnestly.

"Well," Jake drawled, "I've ridden with a lot of good men, but I guess I'd have to say the best was Roscoe Banks. He was a real one. Used to ride for the VB over east of here. That's another big open-range outfit. Runs from just north of the Frisco Peaks to Grand Canyon. Roscoe was the kind of feller you want to partner with. If you told old Roscoe you had a great notion to turn a house over, he'd pull on his gloves and ask you which corner you wanted him to take. He'd charge hell with one bucket of water. There wasn't anything about cowboying he couldn't do and make look easy. He rode for us here a time or two, and once, when they were short-handed, he asked me to come over to the VB and help out. I was proud to go. Hard to find the likes of Roscoe around anymore. He died in 1950, same year as Sam's dad. They were a lot alike, Bob Howard and Roscoe Banks—good men. Roscoe didn't have a family, but if he'd of raised a son, he'd of turned out to be like Sam."

"What's that little low grass that's still green, Jake?"

"Why, that there is filaree. Don't look like much, but there's a world of strength to it. This old dry grama grass is nothing but straw now, but that little filaree is stout. They say it never grew in this country till the Spanish brought in sheep, and the seeds came in the sheep's wool. I wouldn't know about that, but it's powerful feed."

"Jake, this Martin, the feller in the camp we're heading for . . ."

"His name is Martin Yazzi. He's Navajo."

"Is he friendly?"

"Of course he is."

"What I mean is, if he's a Indian, why doesn't he hate us whites?"

"Oh, Christ, there you go with the movies again. It ain't like that."

"Why not? If I was a Indian I'd hate whites."

"Well, I guess I'm glad you ain't a Indian."

"I remember Martin from the branding. He's the big guy with the long black hair that he ties in back with meat string, ain't he?"

"That's him. Now you listen. He don't like to talk much. Don't you go to pestering him with a lot of fool questions. You do and he *will* go on the warpath. We got a lot of ground to cover before the crew gets up here Sunday. Remember, till we move out with the wagon we're in Martin's camp. He calls the shots. You just do your chores. Keep the woodbox full. Help out. Be the first one up from the table. Wrangle the horses. Keep your lip buttoned around camp. When we're out alone prowling around you can ask me all the questions you want to."

"We're going looking for rustlers, huh, Jake?"

"We're looking for tracks. The rustlers are long gone."

"What if they come back? You gonna shoot 'em?"

"Nobody's gonna shoot nobody."

"Can I carry the rifle some, Jake? Just carry it. I promise not to shoot it."

"Hell, no."

"Aw, come on, Jake. Just for a little while."

"No, goddamnit. You're like a accident looking for some place to happen."

"Jake, you think Sam oughta grow a mustache?"

"What for?"

"Then he'd look just like that guy in the cigarette ads. You know, the cowboy that always wears a sheepskin coat."

"Shit."

"No, I mean it. He'd look just like him. Is he real, Jake? That feller in the ads, I mean, do you reckon there really is such a guy?"

"Has to be. They took pictures of him, didn't they?"

"I wonder where he lives. Do you suppose he's a real cowhand?"

"Could be."

"He's always got his rope down, going like all get out after something. Maybe they taught him how to ride and rope, but he ain't a real cowboy. What do you think, Jake?"

"Never thought much about it. But I can tell you one thing for sure: He gets paid a damn sight more for getting his picture took than he ever would doing the work."

"He sure keeps his hat nice and clean. I reckon that must be his go-to-town-hat, like the one you keep in the box. He usually wears a white shirt, too. Ever notice that, Jake? Out there running horses in a white shirt. Must have quite a laundry bill. Yes, sir, soon as I get back from Vietnam I aim to get me one of them sheepskin coats. What kind of cigarettes is it he smokes, Jake?"

"Hell, I don't know."

"You've been here a long time, Jake, has the ranch changed much since you first came?"

"Oh, hell yes. When I got here old Baldy was a hole in the ground, and the moon was about the size of a dime."

"A hole? Baldy? Aw, come on."

"True. And the moon was just a little bitty thing. They growed."

"Aw, stop teasing me. I mean the way the outfit's run. The work and all. Is it different now?"

" 'Bout the same. It still takes a cow and bull to

make a calf, and ignorant people like you and me to look after them. Guess it always will, long as people want to eat beef, anyway."

"But everybody back home kept telling me that there ain't any more cowboys. Why is that?"

"Well, I guess folks just don't know any better. They come driving across country like bats out of hell and don't ever get off the pavement so they don't see any cows or cowboys neither. They come through here like a streak of owl shit through the pines, and since we don't hang out around the highway, they don't think we're here. What folks can't see they say ain't there. We're here, same as always. Been here all along. Holdouts. Aim to be here a spell longer."

"Jake, after we whip them Commies in Vietnam, do you think I can get my job back here?"

"Wouldn't surprise me. Talk to Sam."

"I know I got a lot to learn, but there's nothing I'd sooner do. All my life I've wanted a job where I had to wear spurs."

"Well, you came to the right place. Just see how big a hole you can fill on this roundup."

"How do you mean, how big a hole I can fill?"

"How much country you can handle between riders. Most likely I'll be working with you. Keep an eye on me and whoever is on the other side of you. Cover as much country as you can. Watch how the others do. Think a little bit. You're willing enough, I'll say that, but you're short on patience. I reckon age is the only way you learn patience. Watch the rest of the crew. You walk easy and talk small and some day you may know half as much about the work as most of them forget every day before breakfast."

"Who's likely to be with us?"

"Oh, most likely a lot of the same ones that were here for the branding. Maybe not as many. You keep your eyes open and your mouth shut, and you're likely to learn. Just watch and listen. Take old Boots Taylor. You can learn a lot watching him. He used to be one of the best. He may look kinda funny now with that beer belly on him, but he savvies the cow. He worked here before he got married and went to running his father-in-law's filling station in town. I knew Boots was a real one first time I ever saw him. He buckles his spurs on the inside. That's a sign he was taught by old-timers. In the old days they kept the wide part of their spur leathers on the outside for show and had the buckles on the inside of their feet. You can tell a lot about a man from his outfit. Of course, anybody can put together a outfit, but you can always tell the real hands from the phonies. If a man brags on himself he's likely to be a four-flusher. But if he tells about how he got bucked off by a horse, or outsmarted by a cow, or caught short some way, he's likely for real. Boots is like that. You watch him and me. If you're ahead of us, you're going too fast; behind us, you're too slow. You want to watch Sam, when you can, to learn something about handling horses. He's the best there is, bar none."

"Is Floyd going to be doing the cooking like at branding?"

"I expect."

"Good. I sure liked his chow."

"Yup, he's one the best cooks you'll ever eat after. Used to be a helluva bronc stomper, but he got his back hurt and had to take to bartending. Likes to get out here when he can, but he can't take the work anymore. He ain't drawn a sober breath in six years, but he can cook up a storm."

It was late afternoon when Jake and Will reached Martin Yazzi's camp and corralled their horses. A yearling steer was eating hay in a pen next to the barn and Jake nodded toward it as he untied his latigo.

"Looks like we've got a chore to do this evening," he said. "Beef that steer to feed the gang coming Sunday."

Will flashed his dazzling, ingenuous grin.

"How we gonna kill him?" he asked.

"Never mind," Jake said. "Remember, this is Martin's camp. He'll tell us what he wants done."

Later, when the shadows were lengthening, the three men walked to the pen where the young steer was held. Martin carried the rifle Sam had left with him. Jake had two skinning knives with curved blades and a meat saw. Will was shouldering an ax. The steer got to his feet as they reached the fence and moved to the far side of the pen.

"Looks like he ought to be fit to eat, don't he," Martin said quietly.

"First rate," Jake said.

Martin levered a cartridge into the chamber of the rifle and raised it to his cheek. The short saddle gun barked and the steer dropped to the ground.

"Hot damn," Will exclaimed as Martin quickly went

to the twitching steer and cut a gaping wound in its throat. Dark blood gushed forth and puddled in the dirt. With deft strokes the big Indian widened the gash until all of the arteries and the windpipe had been severed. The steer's sides pumped and air whistled in and out of the hole in his throat.

"You see," Jake said to Will as Martin pulled the steer's head back to open the wound, "you don't want to kill him too dead. You want him to pump all the blood out. He can't feel a thing. You want him unconscious, but not stone dead."

The steer's legs swung feebly as they watched, and the brown dirt around the open throat turned black. When the steer was still, Martin stepped nearer and tried to make the legs twitch some more, but they would not.

"Now the coolie work begins," Jake said, handing one of the knives to Martin.

With Will trying to be helpful, they rolled the steer onto its back and began removing the hide. Will watched intently as they slit down each hind leg on the inside and peeled the hide away. They worked carefully up the belly and brisket, and down the inside of the front legs. As the hide came loose they laid it out, flesh side up, on the ground, and rolled the carcass over on it. The steer was in good flesh and the skin came away easily. Martin cut a small slit in the belly and inserted two fingers pushing away the paunch. He slid the blade of his knife in between the fingers and pushed the knife forward up to the breastbone. Jake worked in the other direction and they were soon able to draw out the stomach and intestines. Jake removed the liver and heart and put them aside. Martin showed Will how to hold the legs while he took them off at the knees with the ax. Jake went to the house and brought back a white-enamel dishpan. He put the liver and heart in it and as Will watched with an expression of wonderment, he carefully dissected a tubular section of the paunch.

"You aim to eat that?" Will asked.

"Damn right," Jake said.

"But it's guts."

"Right again," Jake said, "marrow gut. Tastes just like bone marrow. Best stuff you ever laid a lip over."

Jake continued to rummage in the offal while Martin split the skull with the ax and removed the brains and tongue. They went into the dishpan and Jake added a gland he had retrieved.

"Let's see if we got everything," Jake said, squatting beside the dish pan. "Liver, heart, kidneys," he said, poking each as he named them, "sweetbreads, brains, marrow gut, and tongue. That's the works."

Will stared at the pan with an expression of dismay. "I never knew you ate guts," he said.

"It's sonofabitch stew," Martin said. "It'll put lead in your pencil."

"You aim to make a hand on this outfit," Jake said, "you'll put a lot of it through your system. Meat keeps, but innards won't, so you got to eat them first. Now let's quarter the beef and hang it out to cool."

It was almost dark by the time they had finished and washed up. By the glaring white light of a Coleman lamp Jake showed Will how to cut the organ meat into inch-square cubes and put them to soak in salted water. He browned the pieces of meat in some fat rendered from kidney suet in a black cast-iron Dutch oven, and set aside the brains and sweetbreads. After adding enough water to cover the meat in the pot he tossed in a palmful of salt and chili powder, and put the lid on.

"Let her simmer slow," Jake said. "When the heart meat is tender I'll put in the rest. Tomorrow night I'll thicken the gravy with a little flour, and that's all there is to it. Genyouwine sonofabitch stew. Stop looking so worried, Will. It's good grub. You look like you think it would gag a maggot, but I'll bet you go for seconds. Time you leave this outfit you'll be able to doctor for screwworms all day and enjoy fried rice for your supper."

They ate warmed-over frijoles and panfried steaks with biscuits, and talked about how they would go about checking the river fence.

"No sense in coming in at noontime," Martin said.

"No," Jake agreed. "Best eat hearty in the morning. Our breakfast's going to be plumb used up time we get in for some of that good stew tomorrow."

He winked at Martin, who was clearly amused over Will's discomfort at the thought of eating guts.

"Nothing like a good simmering stew to come home to after a long ride," Martin said.

"Aw, lay off, I'll eat it," Will said as he rose and carried a dishpan of hot water from the stove to the sink and began washing the plates and utensils. On a shelf above the sink was an alarm clock and a brown bottle. Will read the faded label on the bottle. It was Seagram's Seven Crown. The label showed signs of age and was beginning to curl away from the bottle at one corner, but the tax stamp had not been broken and the bottle was full. Below the words AMERICAN WHISKEY A BLEND was a message in script: *A whiskey of distinctive character, smooth, rich, full-flavored without a trace of heaviness.* Martin brought his empty coffee cup to the sink.

"How come you keep that whiskey there?" Will asked.

"Case I get snakebit," Martin said and turned away.

Will saw Jake frown at him so he concentrated on the dishes, and listened as Martin and Jake talked.

"That river fence is tighter than a bull's ass in fly-time," Martin grumbled. "I've seen every inch of it, and nothing came or went that way."

"Well," Jake drawled, "it won't hurt to check it out again. I've got a couple of colts I want to put some mileage on anyway."

"I get mad just thinking about it," Martin said. "Sam must think I don't ride my country."

"No such thing," Jake said quickly. "He knows better. He's purely puzzled, but he ain't blaming nobody. The thing is, Spencer Butterfield is on his way up here from Sonora, and Sam has to at least be able to say that the outside fences have been checked."

"What's Butterfield like?" Martin asked.

"Well," Jake said, thoughtfully, "first of all, he's tough and determined, but he's as fair-minded a man as I've ever known. He's death on cow thieves. I've heard tell that down on his Magdalena Ranch in Sonora they had a lot of that kind of trouble until he just declared war and put a stop to it. He armed all the crew and told them to shoot anybody they caught on their range that didn't belong there."

"You think he'll do that here?" Will asked eagerly.

"We'll soon see," Jake said.

6

SAM WATCHED THE TALL FIGURE striding toward him across the airport tarmac, as the sleek private jet began to roll slowly out to the runway. Spencer Butterfield has the look of a leader, he was thinking. Would he look that way if he had not been rich and powerful all his life? Would he carry himself like that if he were only a hired hand like me?

As Butterfield drew nearer, Sam noticed that his ordinarily stern expression was even grimmer than usual. The thin lips were drawn down at the corners, and a scowl pinched a double furrow of vertical wrinkles between his eyebrows. He wore his customary sand-colored Stetson with its creased crown and very slightly curved brim, a squarely cut forest-green timber cruiser's jacket, brown twill trousers tailored for riding, and plain, but obviously expensive, handmade boots. Dewlaps of skin hung beneath his determined chin, and his hooded eyes peered intently out from under the tilted hat brim. His steady gaze was unwavering, and when Sam was a boy it had made him uncomfortable; now he knew the older man better and accepted examination as he stepped forward and shook hands firmly.

"Morning, boss," he said in his usual greeting, and took Butterfield's suitcase with his left hand.

"Hello, Sam," the tycoon said in his low rumbling voice. "Thanks for coming in to get me. I know how busy you are."

"No trouble," Sam said.

They reached the pickup in the parking lot, and Sam swung the suitcase into the bed. As they climbed into the cab, Sam was thankful that he had thought to sweep it out the night before. He eased the truck out onto the highway and picked up speed. It was a fine day with a breeze out of the northwest, which meant that the good weather would continue. As he drove, Sam described the range conditions and gave his predictions for the weights of the calves and yearlings that would be ready for delivery in the fall. He explained how Jake and Martin Yazzi were going to check the ranch's western boundary along the river for any sign of trespassers. The owner listened intently, nodding punctuations as Sam reported.

"Except for this damn rustling business," Sam said, summing up, "this has been shaping up to be a real fine year for us. How are things on the coast and in Sonora?"

Butterfield leaned back on the seat and lifted his chin. "Dry in Sonora," he said. "I shipped the steers up to California early. We're holding them on irrigated pasture at the San Benito ranch. It's an easy haul from there to the King City feedlot, and I can put them in there as they're needed. The market is way off, but I don't think it can stay as low as it is for long. Beef consumption is up. We'll be all right. Even with the shipping costs, we can put those Magdalena steers in the lot at a bargain and the Rocking R calves and yearlings will have cost us a lot less than the going market price come fall."

Sam studied the road ahead and nodded. That was the way it was supposed to work out, he was thinking: turn out thrifty calves and yearlings here for less than their market value to supply the irrigated pastures and feedlots in California. As long as Butterfield could draw on inexpensively raised stock from his open-range ranches, the Rocking R, here in northern Arizona, and the Magdalena Ranch in Sonora, the California operations could run at a profit. Sam knew that that was how the Rocking R had been conceived by Butterfield back when he saw that the new agrarian laws in Mexico would cut into his vast land holdings there despite his powerful friends in the Mexican government. Sam had heard the story from his father, and from Jake Scott, and once he had heard it from Spencer Butterfield himself when the Baxter Chamber of Commerce prevailed upon the wealthy rancher to address their annual dinner meeting to celebrate the town's founding day.

Sam was uncomfortable in the crowded auditorium. He ran his finger under the unfamiliar starched shirt collar as he watched his employer rise to speak. The room became quiet as the gray-haired, multimillionaire looked out over the audience. Lucy patted Sam's knee and smiled at him. Sam leaned back and relaxed.

"Ladies and gentlemen," Spencer Butterfield said in his deep voice, "I have been asked to talk to you tonight about how I came here forty years ago looking for land, what I saw then, the changes I have observed, and what I see for the future. A tall order, but I shall do my best.

"I came to Baxter in 1924 because I had heard that there was a good ranch which was being put up for sale to settle an estate. I saw the day coming when I would need lots of good rangeland, so I brought the manager of my ranch in Sonora with me and together we rode over what was known then as the Campbell Ranch. We studied it closely and weighed its advantages against its shortcomings. I waited for my *segundo,* José Ortiz, to advise me. He had more cow sense than anyone I have ever known. As we rode he would swing down from his saddle and pick a blade of grass and taste it. He tested the direction of the wind, and studied the clouds. Finally he told me that while he had great respect for the strength of the grass, and the availability of water on the ranch, he was uneasy because there was no high summer pasture. 'This should be fall pasture, *señor,*' he said. 'In the summer the cattle should be on higher ground up by the bald mountain while this grass stores its strength. *Cuidado, señor, cuidado.*' I was disappointed because I greatly admired the Campbell Ranch, but after a little investigation I found that I could also buy the bald mountain and the high ranges around it. I did so at once, and a little later added a big block of desert to the south. Land was cheap in those days, and I had a plan that would require a great deal of it.

"To explain my plan, I must backtrack a little. My grandfather came west in 1857 when he personally surveyed the Butterfield Trail from Missouri to California. He established the first regular mail service to the coast, the Overland Mail, and his stagecoaches made the circuitous trip — it was almost three thousand miles — from St. Louis to San Francisco in twenty-five days. Today highways and railroad tracks cover much of the trail, but in some places traces of it remain. I have walked parts of it, trying to see the land as my grandfather saw it. I have climbed over Apache Pass along the old trail where, a hundred years ago, he had to give his drivers triple pay for every run they made because the Indians were so hostile. I have walked where my grandfather walked, and have tried to comprehend the meaning of the changes that have taken place since his time. I have seen many changes in my own lifetime. A trip that took John Butterfield's stages nearly a month to make now takes only a couple of hours by plane. The all-day buggy journey of my boyhood now takes only an hour by car. But what we have gained has been costly. My plan for the Rocking R involved a reversal of that trend.

"When part of my extensive holdings in Mexico became subject to seizure and redistribution, I knew that I had to find unspoiled land elsewhere. I needed range where cattle could support themselves with a minimum amount of overhead and by their natural increase supply my California pastures and finishing operations with raw material. My theory was that by not trying to take more from the land than it could naturally give, a harmonious balance could be struck. My plan was that nothing was to ever be taken from the ranch that could not walk off it. No timber, no minerals, no oil, no crops; just livestock: cattle and horses. I knew that to succeed I would require a large amount of range. That was what I was looking for when I came to Baxter in 1924.

"What I found were three adjoining tracts of land that complemented each other: the high meadows and tablelands for spring and summer grazing, the lower prairie for fall, and the desert for winter. All together, more than a thousand sections. Over the years we have torn down old fences inside the ranch, and improved the outer fences. We have developed new water sources and storage facilities. By keeping the range open, in a natural state, the cattle can adjust to the seasons, and by never trying to carry more stock than the range can support there is always enough feed no matter what the season. We never spend money on supplemental feed. Our cows make their own living, and we cull out any who do not do well on the feed available to them. We have upgraded the quality of our bulls to some extent, but our cows are all ranch-bred, all products of the Rocking R, and they know how to take care of themselves. We run fewer head per acre than we could, and more bulls than we have to. We cull our cow herd more heavily than most ranches, and we keep more of our heifer calves as replacements. We breed our heifers as long yearlings and get them into the producing cow herd sooner than we would if we followed the standard practice and waited until they were two. Our theory is that if nature has programmed a heifer to breed as a yearling she should have no trouble if she is strong and has plenty of feed available.

"Feed is the essential ingredient. Beef is grass packaged in cowhide. When we run out of grass we will run out of beef, and grass is vulnerable. In my lifetime I have seen fine pasture so overgrazed year after year that the grass has not been allowed to reseed itself, so the weeds and brush have taken over. A range that could support a hundred head of cows will be destroyed by a hundred and fifty head, and will soon be fit for nothing but goats. The West has been plundered by people who thought it was inexhaustible. The hit-and-run exploiters who skimmed the cream and moved on are still among us, but there is not much cream left. What we are doing on the Rocking R, by keeping it natural and not abusing it, is to offer the land protection. When nothing but wild animals grazed it they moved on and gave it a chance to recover and renew itself. Our cattle must do the same. We must not hold them on an exhausted range by hauling hay to them. We must not fence them into an area that needs rest; it should be let alone to be idle and dormant for a while.

"This theory is not prompted by a sentimental opposition to progress or technology. It is simply sound economics. We can produce a calf on the Rocking R for half what it costs on less primitive ranches. We can double the weight of a steer from the Magdalena Ranch during one grazing season on our high range without spending any money on him except for a little salt. Each of our mother cows pays for herself with her first calf, and we can get nine or ten calves from a cow in her lifetime. This was the basis of my plan. I knew that with enough good land the cattle could earn their own living. By always controlling the number of cattle according to the condition of the range we can guarantee that living, and keep the range healthy at the same time. Land health is the extent of its capacity to renew itself. Most of today's small intensive ranch operations are technological dependents. They are demonstrations of the philosophy that believes in improving the pump, rather than improving the well. The West has suffered from that philosophy ever since the first Spaniards came to exploit the region, looking for gold and converts. Since that time, trappers, miners, loggers and ranchers have plundered the wild life, minerals, timber and grass. Today, the federal government owns most of the grazing land and timber in the West and they regulate its use. Most of the ranches as large or larger than the Rocking R depend upon leases of government land. After my experience in Mexico, I decided that I wanted to own my land, not lease it. I do not have to account to anyone for how I use the land, but I know I am responsible to the land itself, and I must not abuse it.

"As for the future I can only say that as long as people eat beef, there will always be a need for open range, and for ranches like the Rocking R. By combining traditional techniques with a new awareness of the limits of exploitation, I predict that, like the Butterfield Trail, the Rocking R will be around for many years to come.

"Thank you very much."

Sam noticed a vapor trail creeping across the deep-blue sky ahead of the pickup and he wondered what it must be like to fly the new planes. The new jets cruised faster than the propeller-driven fighters he had flown could go at their maximum. All that power, and no torque. It must be a fine feeling. Suddenly he realized that Spencer Butterfield had said something.

"What?" Sam said.

"Have you brought in the bulls yet?" Butterfield asked, his voice seeming to roll up from somewhere behind his belt buckle.

"Not yet," Sam said, "but we'll get to it as soon as we get the steers counted. The bulls have pretty much quit the cows. By the end of the month they'll be done with breeding and rested up. Those young purebreds you sent from California ganted up bad at first, but now that most of the cows are bred they're beginning to graze and fill out. Our old native bulls are in good shape."

Butterfield nodded. "Next year I think we should leave the nuts on a batch of the best bull calves and raise them as replacements. A couple of hundred anyway. What do you think?"

"It wouldn't hurt," Sam said. "We're going to baloney a lot of six-year-olds come fall."

"Yes," Butterfield said, "we don't want to let the herd grade up too much. If we get too much purebred in them the cows will get too typy and start losing their instincts. I can tell you, those high-grade cows at San Benito don't make near as good mothers as the Rocking R cows. It seems that those fine-looking prize-winning cows would just as soon orphan their calves as not."

"Our old wild cows will fight for their calves," Sam said. "They may not be so pretty, but they hustle for themselves and they really mother their calves. Our native bulls are rough-looking, but they get the job done. When we first turned them out with the cows they went right to work. Jake showed me one big old long-backed, ranch-bred thing he calls Mussolini. Jake swears that bull didn't eat or sleep for a week after he was turned out. Says that if the big bull was mounting a cow, and spotted one of the little purebreds sniffing around another cow, he would hurry up getting that first cow bred so he could go run the little bull off and get the second cow. Just a big ugly breeding machine."

Far from the highway, up on the tableland to the north, Mussolini lay in the shade of a tree attending to his cud. He tipped his broad muzzle up and closed his eyes as he chewed the undigested grass he had swallowed earlier in the day and had just brought up from his stomach to grind down and reswallow. He methodically slid his huge lower jaw from side to side, grinding and grinding the pulp of grass between his broad back teeth. A red-tailed hawk swept slowly along a thermal above the bull and shrieked a shrill cry, but the bull was indifferent to the sound. Few things disturbed Mussolini now that most, if not all, of the cows in his territory were pregnant and had stopped scenting the air with maddening estrous discharges. He no longer patrolled the range bellowing challenges for all to hear, disturbed by the odor of cows in heat, mounting and remounting the cows who sought him out and some who had not. Now the cows were bred and Mussolini was content.

What he did not know, as he lay there ruminating, with one front leg bent back beside his white brisket, was that soon the men on horseback would appear and drive him and all the other bulls out of the high country. This had happened to him twice before, since this was his third year out with the cows, but he did not clutter up his mind with memories or keep track of the passage of time. His brain was a blank. It was open and receptive to signals from instincts; instincts programmed to respond to such impulses as the warning buzz of a rattlesnake, or the high-pitched bawl of a heifer in heat, or the rumble of thunder in the mountains, which might mean a flashflood. He reacted to such messages without having to pause for thought. Now visceral signals had replaced the glandular drive, and he applied himself to his cud.

When he and the other bulls had been driven up to the high range early in June, the cow odors made Mussolini forget his stomach. A sexual hunger flared up and burned intensely, night and day, seeming to feed upon itself and generating a hot primeval longing. His need was so powerful that the pressure of his passion overpowered all other instincts. Now, almost ninety days later, the cows have been bred and the air is no longer charged with the aroma of their heat.

In many ways, and by almost any standard, Mussolini is very ugly. He carries his huge head belligerently, with his muzzle lifted and his heavy lower jaw thrust out. He is too long in the back, too coarse and rough in his conformation. His widespread, downward-curving horns are too long and the white tuft at the end of his tail touches the ground when he is standing still. The great dewclaws on his ankles rattle as he walks ponderously through the rocks on huge splayed feet. He bellows and moans and grunts as he plods along, occasionally tipping up his muzzle to bugle into the distance, claiming his area, filling the canyons with noise, sending younger, smaller bulls to some less desirable territory. He is primitive and bears little resemblance to the pampered 4-H–project pets seen at fat stock shows with their marcels and pedicured hoofs. Where those bulls have to be led to cows, Mussolini has ranged lustfully uphill and down, randy and rampant, lean and boisterous, planting his sperm, and leaving humped-up cows in his wake.

He does not know it, but his time is nearly up. He has been with the cows long enough for them to come in heat three times. Any that are not pregnant now will be culled out and sold. Soon horsemen will come and rouse him. The number branded on his shoulder will tell them that his usefulness is past and he will find himself in a confusion of pens, with electric prods biting at his ample hams, on his way toward a cardboard box labeled "Bologna." But for the moment, Mussolini rests.

Sam noticed that Spencer Butterfield glanced at the patch of new fence along the highway, but he offered no explanation and Butterfield asked for none. He probably knows all about it anyway, Sam thought. Damn little gets done around here he doesn't know about. I wonder what he would say if I asked him for more money? Not just a raise, a percent of the profit. But how in hell could you ever figure out the profit?

They drove in silence with fence posts blurring by. Sam finally made himself say, "Spencer, I'd feel a lot better if I was putting by a little money, if I felt like I had a future. I don't seem to be getting anywhere. Can we work out some way I could get a share of the profit at the end of each year?"

Butterfield turned toward Sam who stared straight ahead.

"That what's been eating you?" Butterfield said.

"I don't know," Sam said. "It's just that, hell, I'm forty-four, and I don't see much of a future for myself. I can't even see beyond payday."

The older man looked out at the road and then down at his boots. "I was trying to work out something with your father just before he died," he said softly. "It's complicated. Let me think about it."

"You know," Sam said, "I never gave much thought to the future until recently. I don't know why, but I feel like I should have a hole card."

"Mmm," Butterfield growled. "It helps."

Sam felt relieved. He had been dreading bringing the matter up, and even though he had not been given much more than a vague reassurance, his spirits rose.

"Look, Sam," Butterfield said abruptly, "I don't want you to think that I'm making too big a thing out of this rustling business. I've been through it before down on the Magdalena Ranch. Once it gets started it's hard to stop. I was damn near nickeled-and-dimed to death down there, and I sure don't want to have to go through that again. Farnsworth has done a good job, and this county is known as an unhealthy place for cow thieves, but there are things he can't do, so we have to do them for ourselves. You have all you can handle with the regular work, and you've already gotten behind because of this roundup. I've called in some help. Some of my people are checking things out down in Pima County, and I'm bringing a man up from the Magdalena Ranch to help here. He's had experience with this sort of thing, and he'll get to the bottom of it. His name is Luis Pardee. He's worked for me ever since he was a kid, except for the war and a few years afterward. We can count on him."

"Pardee?" Sam said. "Mexican?"

"Half. He was raised bilingual and has done a lot of important work for me in Mexico. He's coming up here and I want you to give him a free hand. He'll know what to do."

Sam nodded. He was vaguely uneasy but did not see how he could object.

"Show him around," Butterfield said. "Give him a string of horses and a camp to work out of. Who's in the Elk Creek camp? Since Jake and the Indian are checking the western boundary, let him start on the east side. Do you think they could have come in from there?"

"I can't see how," Sam said, "but then none of it makes sense."

"Luis will figure it out," Butterfield said. "He's done this kind of work before."

"They used to call them enforcers didn't they?" Sam said. "Stock detectives who tracked down cow thieves. Tom Horn and the like. Well, send him along. Maybe that's just what we need."

As they turned off the highway onto the ranch road Butterfield said, "Have Jake come down to headquarters. I want to talk to him. He's getting too old to spend the winter alone in a camp and I can use him at San Benito after you ship in the fall. Do you think he'll go along with that?"

"I doubt it," Sam said. "I've had a boy with him this summer, helping with the heavy work like packing salt. He swears he's looking forward to winter so he can be alone. And you know how he hates the idea of irrigated pastures and all those fences. The last time he went to San Benito he came back grumpy as all hell."

"I know," Butterfield said, "but if you don't mind I'd like to try to talk him into it."

Sam smiled, thinking that nowhere else would the owner of an operation have to ask his manager for permission to make a suggestion to one of his employees, but that was the tradition, and Butterfield was going by the book, by the convention that requires that the owner never give orders directly to the crew; only the foreman can do that. The owner tells the foreman what he wants accomplished, but never how he thinks it should be done; that would be insulting. Sam knew that Spencer Butterfield was sincere in his concern for old Jake, but he was sure that Jake would insist on spending the winter on the desert with his cows. The last time the old cowboy had gone to the California ranch he swore that he never wanted to go back.

"Damndest place you ever saw, Sam," Jake had drawled, his disgust accentuating the deep wrinkles around his mouth, "one little bitty field after another. Spend all your time opening and closing gates. Them Californios — *ba-keros,* they call themselves — they pack these big, long leather ropes, and they dally every time. Never tie hard and fast. Hell, if a man goes and ropes something, he ought to want to know he owns it. He ought to be tied to it. They do some fancy catches with those old *reatas,* I'll grant, but always stacking dallies, and letting them slip. They've turned out some well-reined ponies, but they use big old spade bits that look like they would half choke a horse. They know how to put a horse into a bridle, but I don't see why they need all that iron to do it with.

They wear big rowled spurs, not like the Chihuahua ones the Magdalena hands wear, but long, drop-shanked things that drag the ground."

It was the night of Jake's return from San Benito and the old cowboy's face was collapsed into a mass of wrinkles. His eyelids drooped. He and Sam were seated at the kitchen table in Sam's house with an almost empty bottle of bourbon between them. Lucy had gone to bed, and Sam could tell by how relaxed he felt that he was getting a little drunk. He poured himself a half shot and pushed the bottle toward Jake. The old man contemplated the bottle for a moment, lifted it, and poured a little whiskey in his glass.

"They eat store bread all the time," Jake grumbled. "There's roads all over the ranch, and camp tenders keep 'em supplied. Bet they wouldn't know how to make a biscuit."

Sam smiled and stretched his feet out. He felt so good, and his affection toward Jake was so strong, that he did not want to end the evening, but he could see that it was past time for them to get to bed. Jake studied his glass, lifted it, and tossed his head back as he drank.

"Bread-eaters, that's what," Jake drawled. "Horse-choking, bread-eating, spur-dragging, dally-weltering, sonsabitches. Get lost in a round corral with the gate shut."

"I'll bring him down this evening," Sam told Butterfield, "but I think San Benito has seen its last of Jake Scott."

7

TRAVELERS CROSSING ARIZONA, far to the south of the Rocking R, who have spent hours droning through the desert's seeming barrenness, blink their eyes in disbelief as the towers of Genco loom ahead like sentinels on the empty horizon. Suddenly, the wasteland of greasewood and yucca is taken over by industry. White cement-block buildings rise up abruptly. Grain elevators stand in tall rows, and wisps of steam puff from smoke stacks that stab into the cloudless sky. As they draw closer, tourists become aware of intense activity: trucks move back and forth inside the high chain link fence, freight cars are bumped and shunted around a maze of railroad tracks, men on horses pace the corridors between the acres and acres of pens, which hold cattle of every imaginable size, color and condition. Even the pure desert air cannot absorb the sweet, heavy odor of the tons of manure being generated.

On and on the travelers roll, past miles and miles of

cattle feeding with their heads beneath bars of pipe above cement troughs, which are continually refilled by trucks with side delivery spouts. It seems to go on forever, but it ends as abruptly as it began at another cluster of buildings of the same cement-block construction as the first, only not so tall. These last buildings house a huge slaughterhouse and packing plant. A terminus in more ways than one. After Genco is passed, the vista is once again unbroken desert, and will remain so for sixty miles. Then a settlement and a row of ancient cottonwood trees mark what once was a stage station along the Butterfield Trail.

To the hurrying traveler, Genco flashes by as an interruption in the monotonous scenery, an anomaly; but it is more than that. Genco is industry. Genco is the factory where raw materials of the West are assembled and packaged and shipped to distributors. It is the equivalent of the oil refinery, the steel mill, the automobile assembly plant, and all the other points at which materials are brought together to be given shape, finished and formed into something usable. Less than a hundred years ago buffalo hunters harvested the herds on the plains. Today the buffalo hunters have been replaced by Genco's computers. But the buffalo hunter is not to be mourned. More often than not he killed for the hide alone and left the flesh to rot. Genco wastes nothing and puts every scrap to use, even down to recycling the urine and manure, refining them into nitrogen, which is steamed and mixed into feed. When this urea meets the bacteria present in all bovine stomachs a chemical reaction takes place that produces protein; manure turns into meat.

Genco can feed 125,000 cattle at a time. The packing plant can harvest 10,000 head a week. The cattle walk in at one end and come out at the other as individually wrapped portions. What began when a cow and bull got together in the wilderness ends here in the din of the killing floor. In between there are many steps in the process. Hundreds of sharp-eyed buyers tour the rangeland and attend the sales to keep Genco stocked. Most of all, they are looking for yearlings that weigh around seven hundred pounds. They are under enormous pressure to find such feeders because Genco must be kept close to capacity to run efficiently and show a profit. The buyers are kept informed by Genco's computers. They are told to a fraction of a cent a pound what they can pay for cattle of all weights and conditions. The computer projects how much feed, at what cost, each category of cattle will consume before they are ready to be killed and cut up. The buyers are never able to offer the ranchers as much as they would like to get for their cattle. For that they are despised. But the ranchers must sell their cattle, so they need the buyers, and they are at the mercy of what Genco's computers say the cattle will be worth a few months hence, after they have converted an enormous amount of feed into flesh and have reached a killing condition. For that, Genco is despised.

If the rancher has feeders for sale that he has raised from his own herd, he has spent a year husbanding them, and the year before that caring for the cows that mothered them, and years before that conditioning his herd. He knows his cattle. They are the end result of his struggle and his dream. Now, because of influences over which he has no control at all, the Genco computer does not think that they are worth nearly as much as he thinks they should be. The cause may be remote: a drought which has raised the price of grain in the Midwest, an abundance of imported beef, an ominous trend on Wall Street. Anything. The buyer and rancher haggle briefly, but the sale must be made because the rancher is not able to convert his feeders into beef. At a time agreed upon, the yearlings are penned, weighed, and loaded into trucks. The buyer telephones Genco and tells them the details of the purchase and when they can expect delivery. An operator punches a code into the computer, and Genco is ready. The destiny of the yearlings has been determined.

One after another powerful diesel tractors pulling slat-sided livestock trailers turn off the highway and draw up to Genco's receiving gate. The driver hands in his manifest, which is scanned by a television camera for relay to the offices high above. The computers match the numbers in their memories and instantly give back an analysis of where the cattle came from, how much was paid for them, what they weigh, what pens they should be sent to, and the code number for the feed mix they are to be started on. Each unit of cattle is given a set of numbers that will stay with them as long as they are inside the Genco chain link fence. This takes a matter of seconds and then the loudspeaker booms out instructions to the truck driver, who shifts gears and moves toward the designated loading chute as the following truck comes up to the receiver's window.

At the chute gates the bewildered cattle scramble down the cleated ramp and are driven by men with buggy whips through the alleys to a holding pen. Here they remain until they can be examined and given whatever treatment the coded numbers indicate they require before they are started on the one-way shuttle that will eventually bring them to the packing plant beyond the vast network of pens. They are whipped and hotshotted into a deep cement trough, which is filled with a gray malodorous liquid. It is so deep that they must swim for a few feet as men above them shove their heads under with poles, to be sure that the chemicals saturate every hair and kill every parasite. On the other side of the trough the dripping cattle are met by men on horses who drive them farther into the maze of iron-pipe pens, by whistling, shouting, and whipping. The yearlings press together, each one trying to burrow into the bunch, tipping up their noses so they can squeeze as far as possible toward the shelter provided by the bodies of the rest. The noise the men make is all around them, and the cattle bawl in dismay. Nothing in their lives has prepared them for this.

At last they are turned in at yet another gate and find themselves alone in a small pen, isolated for a while, quarantined until the computer is satisfied that they have not brought any diseases into the Genco compound. The feed trough has been filled, and as the cattle calm down they begin to eat. That is what they have been brought here for. In the towers to the east the computer has mixed them a formula which will be concentrated and augmented as the days go by. It is a steamed mixture of soybeans, corn, sugar beets, cottonseed meal, hay, grain, antibiotics, chemicals, and stimulants designed to stir their appetites until they are consuming up to twenty-five pounds of feed every twenty-four hours. They will eat under the desert sun by day and under neon lights at night. The strange trucks prowl the alleys between the pens, dispensing the mixed feed through a spout as they creep along the troughs. When his truck is empty the driver returns to the corner of the compound and radios his number to the operators in the tower. A computer feeds figures to the mixer and the hopper above the truck is filled exactly to formula. The hopper is dumped into the truck and the weight is checked and recorded. His radio tells the driver to move out. Day and night the cattle eat. In 120 days a seven-hundred-pound yearling steer fills out to eleven hundred pounds. The heifers are a little smaller, but just as fat.

Fat is the objective. Soft, white fat, which will ooze between the fibers of the flesh and lie in wavy streaks, veins and flecks, like the patterns in marble. Sheets of fat, which will line the interior of the carcass, enabling it to win the grade of Choice. Gobs and gobs of fat, encasing the kidneys and tenderloin so the grade may be raised to Prime and bring many more pennies for every pound. Fat which will ultimately fill the empty scrotum of each steer, making him look as though he had been returned the testicles that had been removed when he was an infant. Fat to make the heifers short of breath and soften every tissue in their adolescent bodies to the texture of soap. Fat that no one needs, but that most people believe to be desirable because they have been told that it is and because they have never tasted beef from a mature animal in good condition. The consumers want fat baby beef. The graders require it. So the lights burn at night at Genco, and the juvenile cattle eat and eat, stimulated by synthetics like diethylstilbestrol, which has been proved to cause cancer. Night and day the trucks crawl along the manger, augering out feed. Since it takes eight pounds of grain to produce one pound of beef, some steers will consume three thousand pounds of the computer's formula. Some may be at the troughs long enough to be fed their own processed manure mixed with high protein concentrates. All of them will die fat.

Week by week, the yearlings grow fatter and fatter, and as they do, they are moved closer and closer to the slaughterhouse at the western end of the Genco compound. Finally, the computer reports that they are ready. Now they must die. Not tomorrow or the day after. Now. They have passed their optimum rate of gain. It is no longer economical for them to continue their twenty-four-hour-a-day consumption. Holding them longer on full feed will not return the maximum profit. So they are moved into a final pen, where there is no feed trough. From there they are marched slowly up a ramp to meet destiny in a long metal stall. One by one, the last thing they are conscious of is a man in a white coat who leans over the top of the chute and presses a stubby rod against each forehead. This is the stunning gun. One at a time the animals drop. The side of the stall is lowered and they slide down to the cement floor to have a chain hooked around a hind leg. A man in rubber boots attaches the chain to an electric hoist and the cattle are raised to a track suspended from the ceiling. They are unconscious. One by one, their throats are cut and great gouts of blood, dark, warm blood, gush forth to spill into a drain in the cement floor. The animals are unaware of the noise of the machinery. They are no longer animals; they are beef.

The carcasses dangle along the track from station to station on this disassembly line. The heads are removed and impaled upon a spike so they can be skinned and have the tongues taken out, the cheek meat cut away, and every scrap of flesh scraped off. Workmen with electric choppers, resembling monster claws, crunch off the forelegs at the knee joints. Skinners skillfully start removing the hides and attach what they have started to a device that peels the hide off the rest of the way in one smooth motion. The hide is dumped onto a conveyor, and the carcass, now bare and glistening white in its coating of fat, is shunted along to a butcher who slits open the belly and lets the offal spill out in a heap. The intestines look like a snarl of gray snakes. With a minimum of deft strokes, the eviscerator detaches the guts from the carcass and sends them on their way down a moving rubber mat to be dissected and diverted to pet-food canneries and called "meat by-products." They are extremely nutritious. The carcass is moved along to a man with a long electric saw, which is hung from the ceiling by a cable and may be raised or lowered. Here, a chain is attached to the other hind leg, and the legs are drawn apart. The huge saw comes down and chews its way through the vertebrae of the backbone, splitting the carcass exactly in two. Now, it is no longer a carcass, but sides of beef. In a very short time the sides are inspected and graded and stamped and shrouded and shoved into cold storage. Later they will be broken up into quarters and then into roasts, steaks, and stacks of hamburger patties. Much of the surplus fat is trimmed off and recycled to be fed to future Genco boarders.

The subject of Genco played a large part in the conversation Spencer Butterfield and Jake Scott had on Wednesday after Sam brought Jake down to headquarters, but neither of them mentioned this to Sam. After making several telephone calls the next day, Butterfield announced that his airplane was coming for him that afternoon and would be bringing Luis Pardee up from Mexico. Sam drove him to the airport and parked the pickup with its nose against the chain link fence separating the parking lot from the flight line.

"Let's wait right here," Spencer Butterfield said.

"We can talk in private, and we'll see the plane when it comes in."

Sam tipped his hat back and studied the row of private planes parked beside the hanger. The two nearest ones were single-engine Cessnas, and just beyond them was a twin-engine Beechcraft. Over to the right, tied down in the high grass, was an old AT–6, a two-place single-engine trainer left over from World War II. The old plane's metal skin was dull with oxidation and one of its tires was flat. Like me, Sam was thinking, it's seen better days, but, what the hell, patch it up a little and I bet it'll still get the job done.

"Let me tell you about Luis Pardee," Butterfield said in his rumbling voice. "When the plane gets here they will just taxi over and I'll get on as he gets off. They won't even stop the engines, so there will be no time for introductions."

Sam turned in his seat and nodded. Butterfield stared out across the airfield toward the purple mountains and squinted.

"His mother was one of the most beautiful women I have ever known," he said softly. "She had all of the classic attributes of Spanish elegance. A small graceful thing with a pale but somehow luminous complexion, a round face and almond-shaped dark, dark eyes that sparkled when she laughed. Her hair was so black that it made her skin look even whiter than it really was."

The older man paused for a moment, squinting at nothing in the distance. Sam was silent. He had never heard his boss talk about any woman with such intensity. Butterfield leaned back and went on: "She was married to one of my mining engineers. They lived in Nogales. Luis was born there, on the American side. His father volunteered when we got into World War I and was killed in France in 1918, when Luis was four. He grew up bilingual in Nogales and came to work for me when he was sixteen. It was just after his mother died. She had evidently been sick for a long time, but she never so much as mentioned it to me. The mining company carried her as a pensioner and she could have gotten medical help. I visited her from time to time, and she was always so vivacious, so gay. But she was very, very proud and I suppose she didn't want to admit that she needed more help. Suddenly she was dead. I brought Luis down to the Magdalena Ranch and my old *mayordomo* took him in hand and made a *vaquero* out of him. When he was a little older we used him as a *pistolero* in our fights with rustlers, and I relied on him when I needed someone I could trust absolutely.

"When we got involved in World War II I told him I could keep him out of it, but he didn't want me to. He enlisted and wound up in intelligence. When the OSS was formed he was assigned to it and spent a lot of time behind enemy lines. He came home in 1946, but was recruited the next year by the CIA. I guess that life on Magdalena seemed dull to him. You understand how he felt better than I. A lot of you boys came back from the war confused about what you wanted to do with yourselves. You went off rodeoing, and Luis joined the CIA. He worked with them for ten years, and then he came home to stay. He doesn't talk much about those ten years, but he did tell me that when he quit in 1957 it was because he had been obliged to carry out an assignment in South America to which he was completely opposed. He did what he was told, then he resigned. I think it was an assassination.

"Anyway, he came home to Magdalena and has been managing it for me ever since. I have complete trust in him and he has never failed me."

"There's your plane," Sam said as a sleek private jet made its final turn and dropped toward the runway.

They went out to the taxi strip and watched the gleaming airplane glide along the tarmac toward them. It swung around and the door opened letting down a short bank of aluminum steps. Butterfield turned to Sam and shook his hand. "Good luck," Butterfield shouted above the whine of the engines and then he strode to the aircraft. Sam watched a stocky man carrying a large valise, and what Sam guessed was a gun case, come down the steps and greet Butterfield briefly. As he came toward Sam, he walked in an easy, rolling gait. They shook hands and turned to watch the steps fold back into the jet and the door close. The plane taxied out toward the flight line and the noise of its engines lessened. Sam turned to Luis Pardee and took the valise from him. It was surprisingly heavy.

"This way," Sam said and started through the small terminal toward the parking lot, where he was surprised to see Red Farnsworth leaning against the side of his patrol car. He introduced Pardee to the sheriff and carefully placed Pardee's baggage in the bed of the pickup against the cab. Red watched him and studied the cases.

"Aim to do some shooting, Mr. Pardee?" Red said casually.

"Come off it, Red," Sam said quickly. "Mr. Pardee is a friend of Spencer Butterfield's, and what he intends to do out on the ranch is his business."

"Of course," Red said. "I was just surprised because there isn't much in season this time of year."

"He can always shoot varmints," Sam said. "We've got lots of them."

Red nodded and straightened up to tower over Sam and the even shorter Luis Pardee. He tipped his big hat back and let a smile stretch slowly at the corners of his mouth, but Sam noticed that the smile did not change the expression around his light-blue eyes.

"Just so," Red said. He reached into the window of his car and brought out an eight by ten envelope. "I called the ranch and Lucy said I might catch you here. These pictures just came up from the state brand inspector's office. They show the blotched brands on those steers of yours after they were clipped. Thought you might like to look them over. You can have these. I've got another set."

Sam took the prints out and went through them passing each one to Pardee.

"Damn clumsy job," he said.

"Real bad," Red said. "Even old Ted Beemer does better work than that."

Sam noticed Pardee look at him quizzically with his dark brown eyes.

"Ted Beemer is our local small-time outlaw calf kidnapper," Sam said smiling. "He and Red have been playing cops and robbers for years. So far I think they are about even. Red has sent Beemer to jail three times, but Beemer hasn't ever been known to buy any beef. He lives on a starvation outfit west of here. All of his cows have twin calves every year it seems."

Luis nodded, smiling a grim sort of smile.

"At home," he said in a soft voice with no touch of accent, "we have a neighbor whose cows seem to always have twins or even triplets, and in the spring one of our good bulls always manages, somehow, to find his way into the pasture where this neighbor's cows are. I asked him once if he did not think it was strange that our bulls only caused *his* cows to have twins, and never our cows. He thought this over and announced solemnly that he supposed that God must favor him since he had so few cattle and we had so many."

They chuckled at this, but Sam saw that Red was still not laughing with his eyes.

"Sam," Red said, "I want to get the state police to send a helicopter up to scout around your outfit. They can see a lot from one of those things."

"Not a chance," Sam said, heatedly. "I won't have it. They'd get the stock so spooked we wouldn't be able to gather them. No, sir. You leave this to me. I'll handle what needs to be done. You're the sheriff. You stick to your business and I'll stick to mine. Mine happens to be the Rocking R. You worry about how they trucked those steers down the highway; I'll worry about how they got them in the truck. I've got my orders from Spencer Butterfield and I'm going to do what I've been told. You send any helicopters out there and I swear I'll shoot the damn things down. Outside the ranch you can do anything you want, but on the ranch I'm in charge."

"Easy, Sam," Red said, "I hear you. No need to get so steamed up. OK, so you don't want any helicopters. But let me tell you one thing, you and Mr. Pardee. This county is run by law, and nobody in this county is exempt from the law. I won't stand for anybody taking the law into his own hands anywhere in the county, and that includes the Rocking R. You understand?"

"Don't mind old Red," Sam said as he pointed the pickup away from Baxter. "He's all right. It's just that he's used to running everything his own way. This rustling business has got him upset."

"I can imagine," Pardee said, quietly.

Sam thought about this man beside him whom Butterfield regarded so highly. In appearance he was unremarkable: shorter than Sam and more muscularly built, with jet-black hair and dark eyes. Hard eyes, Sam thought.

"Well, it's got us all upset," Sam said. "No two ways about it. I'm going to have to tally the steers to see just how many we're missing, so I'll be pretty busy for a few days. I've got a map of the ranch for you, and we've stocked a camp you can work out of. You'll be on the eastern edge of the outfit where the country gets rough. I'll come over in a day or two and see if there's anything you need."

"Fine," Pardee said.

Not much for conversation, are you, Luis Pardee, Sam thought. Well, I guess in your line of work they don't run off at the mouth.

"There's not much I can tell you that might help," Sam said. "I can't figure out how the steers were stolen. I've got good men checking the outside fences. It doesn't seem that it could possibly have been done without inside help, but I know the crew, all of them, and there isn't a one that I wouldn't trust all the way."

Pardee nodded, and Sam decided that there was not much point in trying to force conversation, so he turned his thoughts to the preparations that had to be made for the roundup. But try as he would, he could not ignore the presence of this dark man of quiet confidence beside him. He wondered what it must feel like to have a man in your sights and calmly squeeze a trigger. Sam had shot down enemy aircraft during the war, but that was different, somehow impersonal and remote. Not at all like aiming at a human being, selecting the part of the anatomy you wanted to hit, and deliberately firing. What if some of Pardee's victims had been innocent? He liked the idea of Pardee's presence on the ranch less and less. It seemed to him that Butterfield had forced Pardee on him, and in doing so, had shown a lack of confidence in his ability to get to the bottom of the theft. I'm between a rock and a hard place, Sam told himself. Butterfield and Red are both determined to handle things their way, and their ways are opposite. With all that pressure being exerted somebody's bound to get hurt.

8

FRIDAY AFTERNOON, after establishing Pardee in the Elk Creek camp, on the eastern boundary line south of Jake's cabin, Sam returned to headquarters. It was the scene of great activity. The chuck wagon was being greased and outfitted, horses were being shod and gear repaired. Most of Sam's horses had sound shoes, but the ones that had been brought in from pasture for the extra men were barefooted. Sam knew that he could delegate the chore to others, but he felt obliged to help. It was bad enough that by tradition each hand was expected to keep his own mounts shod, and just too much to ask them to shoe all of the horses for the extra men.

You run a horseback outfit, Sam remembered his father saying, so you have to shoe horses. He went to the corral and picked an easy horse to begin with, one that he knew would not fight—old Brownie. He untied Brownie's lead rope from the corral fence and brought him away from the other horses. Some of the others, who knew what was about to happen to them and were neurotic about having nails driven into their hooves, were beginning to sweat and roll their eyes anxiously. Brownie came along amiably, without any argument or fuss. "Here we go," Sam thought, not daring to count the horses and multiply by four. "Here we go for a first-rate backache."

He glanced at Brownie's feet and estimated the size of the shoes he would need. Since they were not going to be working in rocky or lava country he would not need to leave extra long heels on the shoes. He selected two round front shoes from one keg, and two elongated hind shoes from another. He hooked the shoes into one of his back pockets and stuffed a handful of silvery nails into the other. On a bench in the tack room he found a rasp, a hammer, a farrier's knife, and a pair of nippers. Brownie gazed at him calmly as he returned.

"That's good, old hoss," Sam said. "You just relax because I'm not looking for a fight."

He ran his hand down the horse's front leg and tugged on the tuft of hair that feathered out just above the pastern. Brownie raised his hoof and Sam assumed the angle, bent his head below his waist and flexed his knees. Muscles that he had not used in a long time stretched, telling him where he was going to be stiff the next morning. He placed the hoof between his knees and gripped it securely. Using the curved blade of the knife, he cleaned the grooves beside the delta-shaped pad, called the frog, at the heel of the hoof, and cut away the surface of the sole until he reached new growth. He put down the knife, picked up the rusty nippers, and using both hands, clipped around the horny outer rim, taking off the grown-out wall. He put the nippers down and picked up the rasp, which he pushed across the insensitive bottom of the hoof, until it was worn flat and smooth. Blood was beginning to pound at his temples and he could feel moisture collecting around his hatband. Brownie remained relaxed.

When he thought that he had taken enough of the sole of the hoof off, he put the rasp down and pulled one of the horseshoes from his hip pocket and placed it on the freshly dressed hoof. It turned out to be one of the narrower hind shoes, so he put it back in his pocket and found a round front shoe. Holding it in position, he saw that aside from being a bit too wide at the heel it was nearly a fit. Sam knew that most cowhands learned to shoe horses in the school that teaches, "If it touches in three places it's a fit. Nail it on." Even though he hated shoeing he was determined to do it right. He looked on horses as he did men, and if they were honest with him, he would be honest in return. Not to shoe a horse soundly was not fair.

He let Brownie's foot down and straightened up for the first time since he had begun the operation, and it was a relief. At the massive anvil, mounted on a stump beside the tack-room door, he closed the heel of the shoe a little by whanging it with a heavy, short-handled sledge. Back to Brownie. Up hoof and down head. Brush the dirt off the sole of the hoof and try the shoe again. Perfect. Without releasing the hoof,

Sam dug some of the flat shiny nails out of his pocket and placed them head first in his mouth. Holding hoof and shoe together with his left hand he picked up the light shoeing hammer with his right. He selected a nail from his mouth with the hand holding the hammer and transferred the nail to his left hand. With his hands and knees he held the hoof and shoe together and set the tip of the nail in the second hole from the heel of the shoe. There were eight holes for nails in each shoe and Sam knew that the second hole from the heel was best to start with in positioning the shoe. Slanting the nail away from the center of the hoof he tapped it home with short sharp strokes. The tip of the nail emerged from the outer wall and he broke it off with a twist of the straight claw on the back of the hammer head. He did this automatically as he drove each nail, because even though Brownie was standing quietly, if something should cause the horse to pull his foot away, Sam did not want to be stabbed by the nails sticking out of the hoof.

By the time he had the first shoe securely nailed on and clinched by bending the nails over, Brownie had shifted all of his not-inconsiderable weight entirely onto the leg that Sam was holding up. As Sam rasped the outer rim of the hoof, where it met the shoe, his back and legs told him that he was the old horse's sole means of support. If Brownie did not have the other three hooves off the ground, he might as well have. Sam glanced at Brownie, who was dozing with his head down and eyelids drooping. Without warning, Sam stepped out from under the horse and let go of the hoof. Brownie almost fell, but caught himself and looked around at Sam with an indignant stare. Sam straightened up slowly and lit a cigarette. As he savored the smoke he counted the horses tied to the corral fence and the fact sank in that he had only finished one hoof on his first horse. A cowboy came by on his way to the anvil and said, "Along about now's when I wish I was a truck driver."

The chuck wagon was called that only because that was the function it performed; it was, in fact, a truck. Sam had bought the surplus army truck two years after his father's death, and turned the draft horses, who used to pull the old chuck wagon, out to pasture. Over the years the ugly vehicle with double rear axles and power in all its wheels had been modified and added to until it was a complete mobile kitchen. Its equipment included a butane cookstove and refrigerator, a water tank, and a powerful winch welded to the front bumper. The winch carried a large coil of heavy cable, which could be run out and wound back in to pull the truck free when it got stuck or blocked in any way.

Jake had been quick to register his disgust at the motorized chuck wagon when he first saw it. "Gonna hafta tear up a lot of good grazing to build roads for that monster," he said.

"That's the beauty of it," Sam argued. "With power in all three axles, that baby doesn't need roads. She'll go anywhere you point her."

"Huh," Jake grumbled. "Next I reckon you'll go get

one of them damned calf tables for branding, instead of roping anymore."

"That's an idea," Sam said, to tease the old cowboy. "What kind do you think is best?"

"You get one," Jake grumbled, "you best get one made of wood."

"I never saw a wooden one, Jake, only metal. Why do you favor wood?"

"It'll burn easier."

Sam laughed. "Don't worry," he said. "We're going to go on roping the calves as long as I have anything to say about it."

Saturday afternoon pickups and cars began pulling into headquarters. One of the first to arrive was a rattling relic driven by Ted Beemer. Sam greeted the sharp-featured little man.

"Sure glad you could come," Sam said sincerely.

Beemer looked to one side and shrugged.

"You need the help. I need the money," he said.

Floyd drove in with Boots Taylor, and Sam helped them transfer several cartons of supplies from the bed of their pickup to the chuck wagon truck. Floyd made sure that one particular box was tucked away out of sight in a corner of the canvas-covered kitchen. When he noticed a smile tugging at the corners of Sam's wide mouth, he said, "This cooking's dry work. A man needs a little lubrication now and again."

"Naturally," Sam said.

"Knew a cook, one time," Floyd said in a way Sam

knew meant that a yarn was coming, "up on the ZX in eastern Oregon. Had himself one of those big old-timey, wicker-covered demijohns. Held five gallons. He'd sip away at her day and night. Don't know what was in it 'cause he never offered anybody a taste, but by the breath he had on him, it sure wasn't sasparilla. Never saw him sober, so you couldn't tell when he was really drunk. His eyes were so bloodshot he looked like he had the pinkeye all the time. One morning we came to breakfast and there he was with a lot of toilet paper stuck to his chin. Must of had the shakes something fierce and cut himself shaving. I filled my plate and sat down. The foreman came and sat beside me. 'Think I better take Cookie in to Paisley,' he sez, 'to the doctor.' 'Why,' I sez, 'you think he's bad hurt?' 'Must be,' he sez. 'He lost so much blood his eyes are clear.' "

"Well," Sam said grinning, "if I notice your eyes losing color, I'll give you a transfusion."

"Be sure it's a hundred proof," Floyd said.

9

EARLY SUNDAY MORNING the roundup crew set out from headquarters going north toward the Bill Williams range. Sam Howard led in his blue pickup, which was loaded with bulky bedrolls. Floyd followed driving the motorized chuck-wagon truck with his assistant Dave beside him in the cab. Dave was so pleased to have been let out of jail for the duration of the roundup that he willingly listened to Floyd's endless yarns and anecdotes. The prospect of long hours of hard work that lay ahead did not dampen his enthusiasm because Floyd had promised him a ration of wine at the end of each day of pot washing. Behind the truck came the remuda of horses strung out with riders on the flanks of the herd. At first there had been some confusion as the more than one hundred horses sorted themselves out according to status, but after a few squeals and halfhearted threats they settled down and moved as a body with the younger mounts to the rear and the seniors jealously guarding their places in front. The men gave them plenty of room and let the leaders follow the truck at their own pace.

That night the crew spread their beds on the downwind side of the weather-beaten house that was Martin Yazzi's camp. The beds consisted of several layers of folded blankets and quilts wrapped in a heavy canvas tarp, and extra items of clothing were packed between the layers. Sam and Jake laid out their beds next to one another and talked over the plan for the roundup after supper. First Jake reported that there was no sign that anyone had penetrated the fence along the river to the west, and then he suggested that instead of moving the steers south to the bull pasture to count them it would be more practical to drive them east to Hart Prairie.

"There's the holding pasture over there, Sam," Jake said. "The fence will need checking, but I think it's sound. Since it's higher and been grazed off, the yearlings will be more inclined to drift back over this way when we turn them loose then they would to leave the lower country down by the bull pasture."

Sam nodded and said, "You're right. There are better places for us to camp over that way, too. Blind Horse Springs and Emery Butte. I'll tell Floyd to head that way. We can noon at Wolf Crossing and camp tomorrow night on the north fork of Alder Creek."

Early the next morning, on a low rise of ground in the rolling sea of grass a dozen mounted men clustered around Sam Howard waiting for instructions. They had ridden out from camp before full daylight, and the sun was now just behind a low bank of clouds on the eastern horizon. The backlighting of the clouds created a halo effect of golden light, with a promise of warmth to come. The men were jacketed against the morning chill, some in denim and others in duck. The horses shifted about nodding for rein, and blowing impatient rolling snorts. Sam rose in his stirrups and with sweeps of his right hand began scattering the riders, sometimes in pairs and sometimes singly. He gave them directions relative to landmarks and reminded them of the need for a clean sweep. He unconsciously cast his instructions in terms of requests rather than orders.

"Jake, you and Will want to take the top and work the draws along the boundary fence? Just keep shoving them along east. Let any that want to drift south come on down. Boots, how about you laying off below them and a little back. Watch out for a couple of arroyos up beside Taylor Butte. Martin, I guess you know Alder Creek better than anybody else. Why don't you try to keep sight of Boots and stay just above the creek."

The men moved out one and two at a time, twisting at the waist and raising their rein hands in the direction they wanted to go. There was no waste motion, no sign of haste; it was going to be a long day. Sam watched the riders spreading out on the prairie of yellow grama grass.

"All right," Jake Scott said, bringing his buckskin horse down from a trot to a walk. "There's the fence.

Now you just prowl along close enough to it so nothing will double back between you and it. I'll be down here below you. Look for me once in a while to make sure you're keeping up. OK?"

"Sure, Jake." Will Michaels smiled his unguarded smile. "And if I see any rustlers, I'll rope 'em."

"Now, goddamnit," Jake snapped. "I told you, just leave that rope on your saddle. You ain't gonna see any rustlers, and we ain't gonna chouse these steers. If you so much as knock a fart out of one, Sam'll corncob you. Not only that, he'll dip that cob in turpentine first."

"I know," Will said. "I know. I'll take it slow and easy. But I'm still gonna watch for rustlers. They could be hiding up in those rocks."

"You watch for steers," Jake said and reined the chunky buckskin away. As Will headed for higher ground, Jake rode toward a draw that looked like a place he might go if he were a steer. He let his horse pick their route as he thought back over what Spencer Butterfield had told him about Genco.

"We'll work along down below here," Sam told Hank. "I'll take the outside, and from time to time I'll leave you on your own while I check things. Just watch for steers coming down from the men above us, and keep shoving them east."

Hank nodded and reined in his restless horse. Sam's big bay Quarter Horse, Rebel, pawed the ground, and Sam put his right hand down to the horse's arched neck and murmured to him.

"You know," Hank said, "this country is so damn big it makes a man feel puny."

"Yeah," Sam said. "Every time I see an airliner dragging a con trail at around thirty-five thousand feet I think about the people in it looking down and telling each other about the wide-open spaces below. If it looks big from up there, they should see how big it looks down here in the middle of it."

In some ways Sam was glad he had let Jake convince him that it made more sense to work the steers east to Hart Prairie than it did to drive them south to the bull pasture. The plan was to cover the range in long rectangular blocks, pushing the cattle gradually up to the twenty-four-hundred-acre plateau at the northeastern corner of the ranch. There they could be funneled into one of the smaller fenced pastures and counted as they were let out to return to their regular range. It really was smarter, at this time of the year, to move the cattle to the higher ground, which had already been grazed, rather than take them south into the unpastured section. What persisted in disturbing Sam was the puzzle of how anyone could have stolen any of the steers. He could not imagine any possible way that it could have been accomplished, but he had seen the pictures of the altered brands. Maybe Red was right. Maybe they could spot some clue from a helicopter. Spencer Butterfield would oppose the idea of calling in the law to handle a problem on the Rocking R. He wanted to do this his way; that was why Pardee was here. Sort of spooky, that Pardee. A very hard case.

Sam and Hank rode down from the rise and positioned themselves to cover the lower fringe of the drive. They moved slowly and steadily over the sweeping range. Sam knew that the steers were unpredictable adolescents. Where a smart old mother cow would try to hide from you and make you ride right up to where she and her calf had hung back hoping to be overlooked, a yearling steer might simply throw his tail up over his back and leave the herd for no apparent reason. Once shaped into a herd, cows settle down, knowing that there is safety in numbers. Not yearlings. They let themselves give way to curiosity and vivid imagination, which make them totally unreliable. If they have gotten into any loco weed, they become weird and witless. Sam knew that this was a bad year for the weed, but since there was so much good grass, he hoped that the steers would not be severely affected. Besides, the loco in this part of the ranch was the milder-acting, white-blossom variety, not nearly as mind-boggling as the purple weed. Sam remembered some of the herds of *corriente* steers that Butterfield had sent up from the Magdalena Ranch in years past. They must have had nothing but weed to graze on. They were so hoppy they were impossible. They had trotted this way and that all the way from the pens, where they had been unloaded, up to the high pasture, sometimes stringing out in single file. When they reached the first dirt-tank water hole, some of them plunged their heads into the water up to their eyes, while others stood knee-deep in the shallow pond and simply licked their muzzles, apparently satisfied that they were getting a drink. One steer in particular had amazed Sam. It spotted a juniper on the skyline and made off for it at a dead run. Sam galloped out around him and bumped him back toward the herd, but he would not turn. Each time Sam ran into him, the steer would look off toward that juniper and make for it. Sam knocked him down twice, but the steer simply scrambled to his feet and kept on. Charging up beside the steer, Sam had beaten it across the face with his rope, but the animal only closed his eyes as they galloped along. Finally, another hand had ridden out, and they both roped the loco and dragged him back to the herd. When they took their ropes off, the steer had forgotten what he thought he had seen on the horizon and was glad to burrow into the welcome anonymity of the crowd of cattle.

The weed was hard on cattle, but it was worse on horses. Sam remembered the night his father had come in for supper with the bad news about Blucher.

"I'm sorry, Scout," Bob Howard said gently, "but we're going to have to put old Blucher down. He's weedy."

Sam's twelve-year-old mind could not accept a world without Blucher. "Maybe he'll get over it," he said. "If I keep him in and feed him and don't let him get any more. Maybe he just got a little."

Bob Howard looked his son in the eye and shook his head slowly. "No. He's too far gone. I was coming back from riding the Elk Creek country, and when I was coming through the horse pasture, I spotted him way off, all by himself. He was jogging along with his nose to the ground for all the world like a trailing hound. Just covering country looking for weed. Good grass all around him, and he wouldn't eat a bite. The other horses were scattered out grazing. Old Blucher was hunting weed. I roped him and brought him in. He's down there circling the corral, sweating and nervous. Crazy as a pet coon."

"But we could try," Sam begged. "How do you know he can't get well? I could keep him quiet in the barn. Pack feed and water to him. He could get over it, couldn't he?"

Bob studied the scuffed toes of his boots and shook his head. "Not a chance, Scout," he said. "You would just be stringing out his misery."

"We could try, couldn't we, Bob?" Sam's mother said softly.

"Please, Dad," Sam said with difficulty. He knew he must not cry or even let his voice betray him. He knew that men did not show emotion, that he must not demean himself by any sign of weakness. It was all right for women to weep, although he only remembered seeing his mother cry once when she had burned her hand, but he was expected to tough things out. When he went to bed, he wept into his pillow. He tried breathing deeply to choke off the sobs and lay flat on his back listening to his parents talking in the kitchen.

"Damn unusual," his father said. "A old plug like Blucher taking to the weed like that. It's usually the yearlings or twos that get into it. Blucher's smooth-mouthed; easy twelve, maybe more."

"How do you think he got started on it?"

"Well, you know we've had these late rains. The grama grass is all dried out. It could be that these rains have started a new growth of the loco. That happens. The seed is on the ground waiting for next spring. Along comes all this late rain, and the seeds sprout, so you get a second growth, and it's green and tender. A old horse could get into some of that and decide that it's to his liking. Then he'll pass up dry grass and go looking for more. It's strong stuff. They get addicted to it."

"And there's no hope for a cure?" Sam's mother asked.

"No. Not really. Oh, he might get over being as ding-a-ling as he is right now. We might be able to keep him in and get him back on his feed, but his mind is messed up for good. I've had to ride some weedy ponies in my time. They're purely dangerous. A shadow will spook them. Things will be peaceful one minute, and then all hell will break loose for no reason. I'd never feel easy with Sam riding Blucher."

"It's so sad," his mother said.

"Well, he'll get over it. I'll give him that Snip colt. He's ready for more horse under him anyway. Snip is a smart thing and gentle enough. I've put a pretty fair rein on him, and he's got the makings of a fine horse. They'll learn a lot from each other."

"School is going to start soon," his mother said quietly. "He'll have other things on his mind."

Sam stopped listening. He didn't want Snip; he wanted Blucher. He went to sleep thinking about his old horse and all the things they had done together. He dreamed he was walking in the aspen grove up the slope behind the house. He was leading Blucher through the slender trees, deeper and deeper into the thicket.

Cattle were beginning to bawl in the distance, and Sam roused himself from his reverie. It was full daylight now, and the sky was a vast blue dome, cloudless and infinite. Sam lifted his rein hand, and Rebel leaned forward into a smooth, long-striding walk. Through the day he and the powerful bay horse worked together to press the steers ahead steadily. Occasionally Sam's mind would go back to the shady aspen grove.

Behind the old log house at headquarters the ground slopes up to a stand of aspen. "Quaking asp," they are called by some, *Populus tremuloides* by others. Green-and-silver-leafed in spring and summer, deep gold in the fall, and etched starkly black against the snow in winter, the trees are a testament to time passing. The presence of these poplars means that there is water fairly near the surface here, for they are fond of moisture. They suck the water up their tubular trunks to spreading branches on high, and the branches carry fluid out to the fluttering leaves. As the water evaporates from the leaves, suction is created down the white barked trunk, drawing up more moisture. The leaves take in carbon dioxide on the silver side, and exude oxygen from the bright-green side. Except for the rustle of the leaves, it is quiet here.

Deep in this grove of slender trees with trembling leaves is an open swale of sandy soil. This is the horse cemetery. Some of the veteran horses die in retirement out on the open range, to be gradually disintegrated by natural processes. Others, when it would be cruel to turn them out to die slowly, are led here and put to earth as painlessly as possible, and buried in the sand. Old horses, who once frisked as colts in the wide world of spring mornings, finally end up here. When their legs are too sore to support them, their teeth too ground-down to nourish them, their eyes too dim to guide them, they are brought here gently, sorrowfully, and shot.

There is a knack to shooting horses, Sam thought. There are certain things that you must do, and those that you must not. As you lead a worn-out old horse into the grove, you must make your mind go blank. Wipe away recollection. You must not think of the first time you saw him, fuzzy-tailed and knobby-kneed beside his mother, indifferent to everything except her warm flank. You must not recall the amazement in those deep intelligent eyes when the first catch-rope tightened around that proud neck. You dare not dwell on the stroking and soothing that you lavished on him, trying to convince him that you meant no harm as you saddled him for those first few rides. Above all, prevent your mind from casting back over all the years that he worked with you, always giving generously of his strength and skill: coming down the steep mountain in a rush, without regard to the slashing branches, because the cattle must be turned; laboring through the cinch-deep snow one step at a time because an orphan calf stayed too long in the high country; or charging over treacherously broken ground to get to an open gate before a flighty band of fillies could escape.

You must suppress all that, and much more, as you dig the hole. As the shovel chews away at the sand and your shoulders grow warm, think only of the natural course of time. Do not recall the names of all the good honest horses buried in the grove. Names are powerful. Think instead of the aspen quaking all around you, tolling the seasons. Weed trees, really, not good for much except their beauty. The Indians have lots of legends about aspen, myths of regeneration. Lift the shovel and think about the legends, not about that old wreck of a horse standing there hipshot, with one tattered hoof cocked, his head lowered as though it were too heavy for him to hold it up. Think, as you dig, about why the aspen quake. It is because the stems that connect the leaves to the branches are not round as they are on other trees. They are flexible ribbons, and their flat sides grow at a ninety-degree angle to the flat sides of the leaves that dangle from them. Both the leaf and the long leaf stem are sensitive to the least whisper of a breeze, and as the leaves wind on the flat stems, they show their alternating green and silver sides. Wound like a spring, the stem then twirls the leaf back, unwinding, fluttering it in reverse, whispering, hissing. The heart-shaped leaves spin and spin, flashing, sparkling after every puff of air.

Dig, and think about the vitality of these animated trees, how fast they grow, how easily they are uprooted in a winter storm, how soon they die and are replaced. Think of the deer and elk that browse on their young leaves, and of the rabbits that nibble at their bark. Think of the beaver dams and lodges built from their slender trunks and branches, and of the birds that feed on their buds. Think of the flowers that shoot up at their feet each spring, while they restlessly rustle and whisper above. Aspen are soft and yet brittle, fast-growing and quickly dead, graceful and very nearly worthless. Think about all that, and not about the fertilizer with which you are about to nourish them. Think about the dappled sunlight in the grove and not about the weight of the pistol on your hip.

When the hole is ready, lead the old horse gently to the edge. Rub your hand across the knobby bone above his eye, and down his neck. Speak to him softly. Do not apologize, he has already forgiven you. Then quickly lift the heavy pistol. Imagine an *X* drawn across his forehead from the base of his ears to the center of his eyes. Shoot him where the lines cross, and help him crumple down into the hole. As you cover him with sand, think only about the pain you have spared him, and the long, untroubled rest he has gone to. Listen to the aspen, whispering the names of other horses remembered after death.

Now you may think of all the others. Say their names. Blucher. Sundown. Duke. Chigger. Gotch.

Reno. Harvey. Fudge. Monkey. Cyclone. Whiskey. Buck. All good, honest horses. All gone. Now shoulder the shovel. Shoulder the shovel, and go back down through the shimmering, whispering aspen alone. Dry your eyes before you leave the woods.

Good horses, Sam was thinking as he let Rebel pick his way down a wash. I've sure had my share. It's amazing how much pleasure you get out of remembering good horses. Good horses and good men. Nothing in the world beats being well mounted in good company.

10

BREAKFASTS ON THE ROUNDUP were quiet, introspective meals, with none of the sociability of supper. The men filled their plates and then themselves with purposeful expedition, scraped their plates clean and dropped them into the dishpan of hot water. The horses were held in a rope corral, and one man caught them with graceful backhand tosses as each hand named the mount he wanted for the morning work. On Tuesday morning, the second day of the gather, Jake heard Will call for Beaver, the horse that always bucked him off, and he quickly stepped to the boy's side and said in a low voice, "Change to Kelly. Use Beaver in the afternoon when he ain't so cranky." Will nodded and told the roper to forget about Beaver and to catch Kelly instead.

As the horses were caught and bridled, each man led his away from the corral to be saddled. It took Will longer than it did the others to get his saddle on, so everyone was mounted by the time he put his foot in the stirrup and started to pull himself up by the saddle horn. Suddenly several things happened: Something that looked like a grain sack flew straight at Kelly's head, and the horse shied violently. As Will got his leg over the saddle, Kelly began to buck, and Will struggled to stay on him. He had not gotten his right foot in its stirrup, which snapped up and hit him on the knee, but he knew that Kelly did not buck hard, and as he had a strangle hold on the horn, he concentrated on hanging to it. Riders came in on him from either side, and the end of a nylon rope lashed at his saddle horn, and the hand that was choking it went numb. By pure accident Will felt his right foot slip into its stirrup just as he lost his grip on the horn, and after two more jumps Kelly stopped bucking and ran away with him. He heard the howls and shouts of the crew as Kelly dashed out across the flat, and he tried to remember what Jake had told him about stopping a runaway.

"A horse has to follow his head," Jake had said the day after Kelly had cold-jawed Will the first time. "You watch a horse and you'll see. He leads with his head, getting up off the ground, jumping over a log, turning a corner. So when you've got a green-eyed runaway, you want to bend him back on himself. Not a big jerk, or you'll knock him down. Just leave a lot of slack in one rein and take hold short on the other. Gradually pull his head around toward your knee. He'll start to bend in that direction, and you'll have him circling. Draw the circle smaller, and he'll slow down. It's called doubling 'cause you just about bend his neck double."

Will slid his hand down the left rein and leaned forward as Kelly pounded along with his muzzle thrust out. The boy was not thinking about the gang of cowboys who were watching him or the possibility that Kelly might step in a badger hole. He concentrated on getting a firm grip on that rein as close to the bit as he could. He tightened his hand and began drawing it back. At first nothing happened. Kelly's neck was rigid. Will braced against the saddle horn and pulled again. Gradually he felt the rein coming back, and Kelly's nose came with it. For what seemed like a very long time the frantic horse ran straight ahead with his head twisted back toward Will's left knee, but then he began to swing over to the left, and soon he was running in a wide circle. Will pulled the circle smaller, and Kelly began to slow down. When it was apparent that the boy had the horse under control, Jake rode out from the camp and met Will coming back. Kelly was blowing hard, and his nostrils were flaring, but he was willing to walk.

"What happened, Jake?" Will asked with a frown, stammering slightly as he did when he was excited.

"Oh, some of the boys just jobbed you a little," Jake drawled. "You handled it fine."

"You mean they did that on purpose?" Will asked.

"I reckon so," Jake answered.

"They spooked my horse and hit my hand when I grabbed the horn?" Will's face was registering stunned disbelief.

"Just so," Jake said. "Wanted to see if you'd do to take along. You got to remember, when a man comes out here and takes on a job, everybody just has to figure he can handle it. They don't want nobody among 'em who can't."

"But why do they have to do something so mean?"

"Well, it ain't got anything to do with you, yourself. They'd treat any new hand the same. They each had a hard way to go when they first started, and they want to make sure that you can take it. They want to see if you mean to make a hand. If you got any quit in you, they want to find out about it now, not sometime later when they're counting on you for something and you don't come through."

"But I could've got killed," Will protested.

"Naw," Jake said. "Bucked off is all. But you did fine. All you got to do is outlast 'em for a little while. Pretty quick they're going to be satisfied that you got plenty of try in you and you'll do. Now, this afternoon you're gonna have to outsmart that Beaver horse so he don't buck you off in front of everybody. I'll try to show you how."

The next day, Wednesday, Sam left Jake in charge of the roundup and rode back to the Bill Williams camp where his pickup was parked. He turned his horse loose in the corral and drove south toward a corner of the ranch he wanted to examine. It was where the long-abandoned headquarters of the original Campbell Ranch had been, and at one time a road had led from there out to the highway. If someone had been able to get a truck in over the old road, they could have taken the steers out that way, but God alone knew how they could have gotten the steers way down there.

As Sam drove, he reviewed his problem, as he had done so often during the recent days and nights. He was no nearer a solution than he had been at the beginning. By the time he reached the decaying log structures which had been the Campbell headquarters, he felt even more confused and frustrated. He left the pickup and walked around the outer edge of the clearing, where stately pine trees swayed in a gentle breeze. His eyes were on the ground, and when he came to the remnant of a road, he turned down it and entered the forest, where it was dark and cool. The floor of decomposed pine needles was soft and aromatic, and as he walked along the long unused road, which led to the boundary fence, he remembered one week in a fall before the war when he and Red had camped here and hunted these woods for mule deer. He remembered the big gray bucks bounding away through the trees, shaking the hollow pumice earth beneath the needles and duff as they ran in stiff-legged jumps. You would see a flash of motion and then hear thunk-thunk-thunk as a buck got up out of his bed and moved down the slope. He and Red knew that the deer usually circled and came back around down wind from their bed-ground, if they were not too alarmed, so the boys would split up to intersect the circle, and if the buck proved to be particularly large, shoot it. They could afford to be choosy because the mule deer migrated through this area by the hundreds. They fed on the sweet little piñon nuts and ferns at that time of year, and their flesh was delicious.

Sam came to a large windfallen pine down across the road, and as he made his way around it, he knew that no truck could have come this way. When he reached the boundary fence, he climbed it and went a little farther just to satisfy himself completely. Suddenly he caught a glimpse of something moving just ahead, and he stepped behind one of the big rough-barked trees. As he peered around the pine, he saw a figure emerge from a thicket of mountain laurel. It was Red Farnsworth. Sam let his breath out and stepped from behind the tree.

"Hey, Red," he called and saw the big man stop suddenly. "Up here. It's me, Sam."

They met on the overgrown road and sat on a fallen tree to talk. Red explained that he had remembered this corner of the ranch from their hunting trip and he had come to see if it was possible to negotiate the old road.

"I had to leave my car back a ways," he said. "Lots of buckbrush and mountain laurel grown up across the road, and some young trees standing right in the old ruts. Nothing been in or out this way."

Sam nodded and said, "And the fence along the river has all been checked. Nothing went out over there."

Red pushed his Stetson toward the back of his head with one large freckled finger. "Sam," he said, "you aren't going to like hearing what I've got to say, but you better listen anyway. I've studied this thing from all angles, and there is just no way that those steers could have been hauled off your outfit without help from the inside."

"I know it looks that way," Sam said, "but I don't know who to suspect."

"Let me come up and talk to a few of them," Red said. "I'm used to finding out things by asking a few questions. That's my line of work."

"Not yet, Red. Not till I've got more to go on."

"Listen, goddamnit, I've got good reason to believe that this isn't just some small-time thievery that you and Butterfield's gunman can cope with."

"What are you talking about?"

"I'm talking about a pattern of cattle thefts all over the state," Red said heatedly. "I'm talking about reports of several carloads of missing cattle. I don't know what it adds up to yet, but I don't think they are just coincidental. All I want is a chance to ask a few questions. I'm not going to lean on anybody."

"Who would you start with?" Sam asked.

"Martin Yazzi, I guess."

"Because he's got a record?" Sam said. "That's the cop in you. Just because he did some time in prison you're suspicious of him. Hell's bells, Red, Martin hasn't been off the ranch for over five years. How could he have had anything to do with it?"

"It's not just because he's done time," Red protested. "How do we know that he didn't get to know somebody in prison who's into cow stealing now? How do we know for sure that he hasn't been off the ranch? He could have ridden in from camp without your knowing about it."

"Is that what being a cop does to you?" Sam asked. "You get to be suspicious of everybody and start to see spooks?"

"Maybe," Red said. "Maybe, but I've been right more often than I've been wrong, and I aim to break this case one way or another, with or without your cooperation."

They parted on that note and Sam began the long drive back up to the Bill Williams camp. Along the way he pondered his problems. He really hated opposing Red, but he knew that Butterfield was determined that the Rocking R would never depend upon outsiders for help. Red was all right. Sure, he was used to running things the way he must have run his platoon in the Marine Corps, but Butterfield had more power than Red ever would. Sam remembered when a young politician had angered Spencer Butterfield by proposing a per capita tax on cattle shipped out of the state. The rancher had been furious when Sam telephoned him about it.

"That boy needs to be taught a lesson," Butterfield growled, and shortly afterwards the young politician came up against an extremely well-financed opponent who campaigned against the tax proposal and won the election. The young politician's party dropped him like a bad habit, and he was never heard from on the political scene again. But Sam knew that Red had better sense than to buck Spencer Butterfield. He could stop worrying about Red and think about his own situation. He was not sure where he stood with his boss now. Ever since Pardee's arrival Sam had felt increasingly resentful that Butterfield seemed to have more confidence in Pardee than he did in him. Christ, Sam thought, I'd a lot rather have Red up here looking into things than that executioner. But Red was dead wrong about Martin; he just didn't know the man. It was probably just that Red was so used to dealing with people who had broken the law that he suspected everybody of being capable of anything.

But Sam had to admit that it was mechanically possible. If anyone could have gotten steers across the river, it was Martin. The big Indian knew every crossing with its shifting beds of quicksand. He was brave enough to try anything, and smart enough to make it work. Jake was just as likely a suspect from Red's point of view. The old cowboy had the know-how and the ability to bring it off. And what about Hank? Lucy had said he made her uneasy; well, he made Sam sort of uncomfortable too, but that was no reason not to take him at his word. Perhaps he *had* just turned up at this particular time after all these years. But was he really as unskilled at ranch work as he claimed, or was that just a pose to divert suspicion from himself? I'm getting to be as bad as Red, Sam thought. Pretty soon I'll be wondering if little Pauline Begay stole those steers.

By the time he had driven to the Bill Williams line camp and saddled his horse, it was growing dark. The sun was easing down behind the western mountains, tinting the dome of sky with streaks of red and purple, and all that was left of the day was yellow light beyond the jagged horizon. Sam stepped up into the saddle and loped his horse toward the dark eastern plain. The steady beat of the smooth gait had a soothing effect, and by the time he reached the roundup camp, he was feeling better. Floyd warmed some supper for him, and Jake gave him a progress report while he ate.

"We've about got her whipped," the old cowboy said. "Another couple of days should do it."

11

FRIDAY MORNING Jake Scott woke up back in his cabin. He was bone tired. His bad hip hurt, and his arms felt very heavy. A man has a right to be tired at night, he thought, but it's a helluva note when he's wore out first thing in the morning. Covered a lot of country yesterday.

The day before, Jake had left the roundup at Sam's request that he check the fence around the holding pasture on Hart Prairie. Since it would take him all day to ride the fence Sam suggested that he lay over at his regular camp and rejoin the roundup the next day. This had given Jake the time he needed. As he rode east ahead of the crew he was able to gather a herd of fifty steers and drive them to the fence above Cottonwood Canyon. He cut a gap in the fence and shoved the steers through, but the light was fading before he had gotten the yearlings all the way to the bottom of the rough trail, where he knew there was a spring. When the roundup was finished he would return and push them all the way down. Now he had to rejoin the crew.

He found half of the men driving the last of the steers toward the Hart Prairie gate. Sam and the rest of the crew were making a final check of the open range to be sure that all of the yearlings had been picked up. At supper there was more than the usual amount of conversation, and most of it centered around what was going to take place in Baxter after the steers were counted and the men returned. It was good-natured talk with a lot of kidding thrown in; the men all knew that they had come out here to do a job and that the job had been well done.

"My old lady is gonna catch hell," Boots Taylor said, as he helped himself to a second huge plate of chili. "She don't make chili near as good as Floyd."

"My woman's gonna catch it too," Ted Beemer said, "but not 'cause she can't cook. I need some loving."

"You ain't gone long without it, Ted," Jake drawled. "Look at Martin here. He ain't been to town since he hired onto the outfit better'n five years ago."

Beemer shook his head, saying, "I can't help it. I got to have it regular. Right now I got a case-hardened, drop-forged, blue-steel pecker. Tomorrow night I aim to wear it down to a nub."

"Somebody ought to go warn his wife."

"Yeah. Let's do that."

"Ted'll get home and find her up on the roof with a rolling pin to fight him off with."

As they finished eating, the men scraped their

enamel plates clean and dropped them into the steaming dishpan, saying, "Thanks, Floyd." "Good chuck, Floyd." "Much obliged." "Them biscuits are so light they need holding down, Floyd." "You sure got a good do on the chili."

Over a last smoke or chew for the day, they swapped yarns and reminisced while bugs bumped against the hissing Coleman lantern.

"The wind blows so hard and steady up there that everybody leans against it. One day the wind quit all of a sudden and they all fell down."

"He has this sign on his gate that says: Trespassers will be shot at and if missed will be prosecuted!"

"He told me he worked on a outfit up north one time away back. Englishman owned it. Said one day him and the foreman was talking when another Limey drove in looking for the owner. This one gets out of his big old car and says, 'Is your master here?' The foreman gives him a long level look, spits on the ground, and sez, 'The sonofabitch ain't been born yet.' "

"I've wore Chihuahua spurs ever since I was a little bit of a button. My daddy gave me my first pair. He always said, 'You don't need to poke a hole in a horse. Long as he knows you've got 'em on, if he ain't been dead more than three days, he'll give you his undivided attention.' All I got to do is shake them big old rowels, and a horse'll hunt cattle like a dog hunts rats."

The next day, with Sam on one side of the gate and Jake on the other, the crew funneled the steers through to be counted. Jake used a short stick he called a tallywhacker, which he tapped against his saddle horn as the steers trotted by. He cut a notch in the stick for every hundred. Sam tied a knot in his pigging string. From time to time they would signal the men to slow the stream of cattle. When the last steer hurried by, trying to catch up with the rest, Sam took a small notebook out of his shirt pocket and checked some figures in it. Jake counted the notches in his tally stick.

"The way I make it," Sam said, "we should have fifty more steers than we have."

"My count shows three thousand two hundred and eighty," Jake said, and Sam nodded.

"We're shy fifty," he said. "How the goddamn hell did they get them out of here?"

Jake shook his head, and Sam said, "Son-of-a-*bitch!*" so explosively that his horse danced sideways a few steps.

As they rode back to camp on Saturday, in the soft summer twilight, Sam told Jake about the arrival of Luis Pardee and that he would be living in the line camp on Elk Creek, south of Jake's summer camp.

"He's going to be prowling around your country, Jake," Sam said. "I don't much like the idea, but Butterfield is set on it. You might look in on him and give him an idea of the lay of the land. I gave him a map, but you can tell him more than it can. And Jake, make damn sure he knows that you're going to be out riding your country — you and Will. I'm nervous about him having an itchy trigger finger."

"Don't worry, Sam," Jake said. "I ain't lived this long by being careless."

"Yeah, but what about Wild Bill?"

"Well, he's another story," Jake drawled. "Maybe I could send him down to headquarters till this blows over."

"Do that," Sam said.

Sunday morning the roundup camp was broken, and Jake and Will rode back to their cabin in the pines to find Luis Pardee waiting for them. While Will turned the horses out to pasture and fed his wrangle horse in the corral, Jake and Pardee talked. During supper Will could hardly take his eyes off the darkly gleaming rifle Pardee had brought in and leaned against the wall. The boy longed to pick it up and look through its telescope sight.

"Is that a special kind of gun, Mr. Pardee?" Will asked, nodding toward the rifle. "It don't look like Jake's."

"Yes," Pardee said in his soft voice. "It's sort of special. It's been worked over some. The barrel was shortened to make it easier to carry horseback. The handle on the bolt was bent down and flattened so it fits in a scabbard without much of a bulge. The scope is adjustable, and it really brings things up close. It will hit anything I can see to point it at."

"It sure is pretty," Will said admiringly.

"The boy's gun-crazy," Jake said.

"In October I'm going to be eighteen," Will said. "I'm going to join up and go to Vietnam soon as I can."

Pardee's face softened and an expression of sorrow drew at the corners of his mouth.

"Don't be in a hurry," he said quietly.

"I can't wait," the boy said. "They'll likely quit fighting afore I get there if I don't hurry."

Pardee shook his head and rubbed the palms of his hands down his thighs.

"He's hell-bent to get himself killed," Jake said. "Bound and determined."

"I ain't aiming to get myself killed," Will protested. "I'm gonna do the killing. I'm gonna get me one of those machine guns, and a big load of hand grenades, and a automatic pistol. I'll just mow 'em down."

"Where did you get the idea that you're going to enjoy killing people?" Pardee asked quietly.

"The movies," Will said smiling. "John Wayne, Randolph Scott. They just shoot and shoot and have a high old time."

When Sam and the extra hands returned to headquarters on Sunday afternoon, Sam paid them and thanked them for their help. Then he called Spencer Butterfield and told him the results of the tally.

"We're out fifty head, boss," Sam said into the telephone. "No two ways about it. I put Luis Pardee in the Elk Creek camp, and he's prowling around over there. I just hope to God he doesn't shoot anybody."

"Luis is not excitable, Sam," the ranch owner said. "He knows what he's doing."

"I hope so," Sam said. "Red Farnsworth sized him up at the airport right after you left. He made it plain that he doesn't like the idea of us taking things into our own hands. He wants to bring in a helicopter and the state police."

"You tell him we can handle this," Butterfield growled.

"I did," Sam said, "but it didn't go down very well."

"Do you want me to call him?" Butterfield asked.

"No. I can handle Red," Sam said. "He knows we don't want him snooping around out here. But if Pardee shoots somebody, it's going to mean trouble. This isn't Mexico, you know."

"Stop worrying about Luis," Butterfield said.

Sam called Red and told him about the fifty missing steers.

"Well," Red said, "we know where fifteen of them are. Now all we have to do is locate the other thirty-five. When we find them, we may just get the low-down on how they were stolen. I'll get on the radio."

After supper that evening Hank suggested that he and Sam should drive to Baxter.

"I feel like walking on some pavement and leaning on a bar," Hank said. "After a week in the wilderness I'm ready for town."

Their first stop was The Homestead, where Perry Jefferson greeted them, his slicked-back hair gleaming.

"What did you do to old Floyd, Sam?" the bartender asked. "He came back and went straight to bed."

"We kept him pretty busy," Sam answered. "You know what they say: Cowhands work from can see to can't see, and the cook works before and after."

Sam and Hank stood at the bar beneath the horned heads of the mounted animals. Men came and went, and several stopped to say something to Sam, who always introduced Hank as an old friend from his rodeo days. They drank slowly but steadily.

"You sure got yourself one fine woman," Hank said.

"Didn't I," Sam answered.

"I guess I never will figure women out," Hank said, staring at the heavy shot glass as he turned it slowly. "Been married to two of them, and didn't ever even understand them. First one was a tall, skinny thing. Looked a lot better with her clothes on than off. She liked to party. We had some wild old times, I'll tell you. She could drink like a man. I woke up one morning with a head like a marble gravestone and found a note saying she had left. A while later her lawyer sent some papers to me in care of the RCA, saying if I signed the papers and sent them back, I'd be divorced. So I did, and that's the last I heard of her. I haven't got the least notion of why she left, where she went, what went wrong, or anything.

"The second one was a cute little thing. She liked the idea of being married to a double-tough, triple-distilled bull rider. I bought a little house trailer and used to drag that thing on down the road from one rodeo to the next. Lord, that was a pain, pulling that trailer, but she wanted to make the circuit with me, and it was a lot cheaper than motels. Along about then money got to be a problem, so I had to put up with the trailer. I hurt my knee pretty bad and wasn't winning anything for a spell. I'd tape that leg to a fare-thee-well, go out and get down on a bull that I knew I could ride, a bull I'd made big wild winning rides on before I got hurt, and when they opened the chute, I'd have my spurs buried in him in a death grip. The trouble was, I didn't have any strength in that right leg at all. That old right spur would come unstuck, and away I'd go.

"It hurt like hell trying to hang on, and it hurt getting homesteaded. I'd get my head punched into the fairgrounds and go back to the trailer to soak my knee. I was crippling around for quite a while. It made me grouchy. Sue, my wife, she took to complaining about us not having any money, about being cooped up in the trailer. I got sore and told her to go on out if she wanted to. I had to rest my leg. She went.

"It got so we argued a lot. She'd storm out and not come back till all hours. I'd get mad. Then one day I was hurting so bad I just had to tell them to turn my bull out, and I went back to the trailer and found her in bed with a friend of mine. I drug him out of there, and bad leg and all, I was just about to raise lumps all over him when he told me he wasn't the only one. Said Sue had been screwing the socks off of just about everybody. He gave me a dozen names. Sue admitted it. Said she hated me and was getting back the only way she knew how. I was ready to kill her, but then I figured she just wasn't worth it. I got in the car and went away. I bought a bottle of tequila and got drunk clear through in a very short space of time. I stayed off the circuit for the rest of that year. Got a job handling stock at a auction yard and sulled around. I felt like I couldn't face any of the guys I knew had screwed Sue. Didn't think I could ever go back to rodeoing. Damn near went crazy. Used to lay in my bed at night going over the list of names.

"The next spring I heard that she'd been killed in a car wreck. Out joyriding with a bunch of drunks and went off a bridge. I was glad. I was glad and sorry. Sorry I'd never get to do her like she did me, glad she was gone. I still get mad just thinking about her, but I don't think about her much anymore. Those old boys she was playing around with have all quit rodeoing, so I don't see them any. I'm the only one still on the circuit. I came back to it after she got killed. After I fist-whipped a couple of her old pals, I felt better, but she sure cured me of the habit of getting married. Anymore I just go for one-night stands or whorehouses. Speaking of which, the boys were telling me that you've got a pretty good one here in Baxter. Think we could try it out?"

"Sure," Sam said. "It's just around the corner."

In the pickup Hank said, "That Indian girl, Pauline. She's a pretty little thing. You ever slice yourself a sample?"

"No," Sam said. "She's almost like family. She and Lucy are close."

"That's too bad," Hank said. "She's toothsome."

After introducing Hank to Mattie at the front door, Sam went to the bar, where he was greeted by Oscar, the bartender-bouncer of the establishment. Sam took a stool next to Jerry Whalen, Red's deputy. Even in civilian clothes Jerry looked as if he were in uniform. His white shirt was starched and pressed, which was not exceptional, but his Levi's were too. He sat very straight on the barstool and tried to look tall.

"You come up with any notions about how your steers got stolen?" Jerry asked, and Sam shook his head.

"No," Sam said, "but I know fifty are missing."

"Hmmm," Jerry said. "That's a tidy piece of change. More than I make a year. You offering a reward?"

Sam shook his head. "Not so far."

"Might help," Jerry said. "Might get folks that saw something suspicious to come in and tell us about it. Somebody coulda seen something, but they just don't think it's worth getting involved unless there's something in it for them."

"I'll talk to Red about it," Sam said.

"Well, just don't say it was my idea," Jerry said. "He'll think I was trying to cut myself in on it. I've never seen him so grouchy as he's been lately."

Sam saw Mattie come in and sit at a table near the doorway. He crossed the room and joined her.

"How are you?" he asked as he sat down.

"Better than the last time you saw me," Mattie said, automatically smoothing her dark shiny hair. "I don't remember when I've been so scared."

"I don't wonder," Sam said. "I was sort of spooked myself. That cannon of Red's makes a lot of noise. He once told me, 'It's good for shooting cars.' I got this picture of him and a car facing each other on Main Street at high noon."

"He's upset," Mattie said quietly.

"Over the shooting?"

"That," Mattie said, "and the way all of the prim and proper types started agitating to close down the houses. As if it was our fault that we got held up."

"That'll blow over," Sam said. "It comes up every now and then, but it always blows over. I remember once, back before the war, when old Jess Rainey was sheriff, a bunch of Bible pounders stirred up a fuss. Jess pretended to agree with them. He told them he'd take action. What he did was go around and persuade all the girls to take a two-week vacation. The houses were closed, and when the girls came back, they quietly went to work, and it was business as usual."

"I sure hope you're right," Mattie said, looking worried.

"Relax," Sam said. "Red knows how to handle people, just like Jess Rainey did. As a matter of fact, Jess was always Red's idol. I think Jess had more to do with shaping Red's personality than even Red's father did. He told me once that when he has a tough decision to make he always asks himself how Jess would have handled it. Like the time Red went into the empty movie house in the dark and brought those three would-be bank robbers out. That was just how Rainey would have done it."

"I never knew Sheriff Rainey," Mattie said, "but Red has told me about him."

"The older Red gets the more he acts like Rainey,"

Sam said, smiling. "I watched Red talk to an Indian boy who had gotten in some trouble the other day, and he reminded me of Jess. My father used to tell about how Jess stopped Ben Beemer, Ted's dad, one time back in the depression days when money was scarce. Ben was the local bootlegger, but Jess left him alone as long as he did his business quietly. He sold stove wood too. He'd keep Ted home from school to help him sometimes. Half the folks in Baxter bought their wood from him, and the ones who couldn't afford beef would order a buck from him from time to time. Jess knew that Ben was killing deer out of season, but he looked the other way because times were hard. Well, this day, when my dad was talking to Jess, Ben came by with a wagonload of wood. Jess stopped him to talk about something. Maybe to order some whiskey. After a little while my dad says he noticed blood dripping from the bottom of the wagon onto the street. Jess saw it too and said, 'Ben, you better get that wood where it's going before it bleeds to death.' "

Mattie smiled and said, "That sounds like something Red would say."

The smile faded, and she looked around the room. "Sam," she said, lowering her voice, "I don't know if this will be of any help or not, but last night two men I'd never seen before were in here, and I heard one of them say something about picking up a load of Rocking R steers for Genco. What's Genco?"

"That's a big feedlot and packing plant down south," Sam said, "but we've never sold them any cattle."

"Well, they sounded like they were expecting to get

some. I couldn't hear everything they said, but it seemed to me that they were waiting to be told when the shipment would be ready."

"Was somebody at the ranch supposed to contact them?" Sam asked, frowning.

"I think so. But, Sam, I can't be certain."

Sam nodded.

"Listen, Mattie, if either of those guys comes in here again, I want you to call Red right away. All right?"

"Sure, Sam," she said and nodded toward the bar. "Jerry hangs out here a lot. Should I just tell him?"

"Not on your life. You just slip upstairs and call Red. This is too important to trust to Jerry. What did these guys look like?"

"One of them was dressed like a truck driver: T shirt, jeans, and boots. The other one was an inside man. His nails were manicured, and he wore dark glasses. Reminded me of the mobsters you see around Vegas: expensive shoes and a couple of big rings."

Christ, Sam thought, that's all I need: Somebody on the ranch in cahoots with the Mafia.

"I'm going to have to sort this all out," Sam said, and looked up to see Hank standing at the bar. "Thanks, Mattie. That's something to think about."

He went to join Hank and realized that he was getting high. He felt very relaxed, and that meant that it was time to go home. He ordered another drink and saw one of the girls come in and whisper to Mattie, who rose and followed her. When Sam and Hank finished their drinks, they started toward the front door.

Sam glanced at a dark stain on the rug at the foot of the stairs where the body of the holdup man had sprawled. Mattie came down the stairs and beckoned to him to follow her down the back hall. She came around Sam and stood with her back toward Hank, who had remained in the front hallway. Sam saw that she was angry. Her handsome face was drawn, and her full lower lip was pressed into a thin line.

"You get that long drink of water out of here, Sam," she said in a low voice between clenched teeth. "Get him away, and don't ever bring him back. I don't know how good a friend of yours he is, and I don't care. All I know is that he got very rough with Peggy, and if I ever see the sonofabitch again, he's going to regret it."

"Christ, Mattie," Sam said. "I'm sorry. I had no idea. I'll give him hell."

"You just do that," Mattie said, and stepped past Sam toward the back of the house.

As he turned the pickup east, pointing it toward the ranch, Sam said, "Feel better?"

"You bet," Hank said. "That's just what the doctor ordered. How come you weren't having any?"

"Well," Sam said, "I guess I get all the sex I need at home."

"Oh, come on," Hank said. "Come on."

Sam felt confused and uncomfortable. He did not like talking about personal matters.

"Well," he said, "I'm married, you know. It may be old-fashioned, but I just don't believe married men should go tomcatting around."

"You mean," Hank said in amazement, "that all the time you've been married you never once tried a little strange stuff?"

"Nope," Sam said.

"I'll be go to hell."

"Look," Sam said. "What other people do is their business. I just have to live up to what I expect of myself, that's all."

"How come they know you so well at the whorehouse?"

"Oh," Sam said, "I've known Mattie for years. Her place is sort of like a club, where you stop by for a drink and some conversation, as much as anything else."

"I favor the 'anything else' part of it," Hank said.

"I wouldn't go back, if I were you," Sam said.

"Why not?"

"Mattie's burned up because you got rough with Peggy."

"Peggy?" Hank said. "The girl I had? Aw, hell, I didn't really hurt her. Besides, she's only a whore."

"Well," Sam said, "you better not go back. Oscar, the bartender, keeps the peace there, and he has been known, as they say, to inflict great bodily harm on anybody that gets out of line."

Hank gazed glumly out into the night for a few minutes, and then he said, "Goddamn women. They'll always get you into hot water. Seems to me I been walking around with a hard-on most of my life, trying to find something to do with it. Chasing women like a damn billy goat. Spending my money on them, lying to them. That's one good thing about whores—you just pay them. You don't have to tell them you love them. All the chippies around rodeos, they want you to tell them you love them. As if that had anything to do with it."

12

MONDAY MORNING Sam drove to Pardee's camp to tell him the results of the steer tally and to make sure that he knew where he might come across Jake on the prowl. As he steered the pickup into the sun, he went over what Mattie had told him the night before. The suggestion that someone on the ranch might be connected with the theft of the yearlings was something he still resisted. It seemed totally wrong, but there it was. Sam remembered an old cowboy he had gone to visit in a nursing home, one who had ridden for the Rocking R until his health failed. The old man's eyes were cloudy, and his hands trembled, but his voice was firm as he drew forth one recollection after another. Sam sat in a chair beside the bed and listened because it seemed important to the old-timer. His name was Tyler Taylor, and Sam could remember when he had been strong and supple. Sam knew that Tyler needed someone who could remember him that way, so he sat by the bed and listened. The old cowboy spoke cautiously, as though he held words in high regard and was careful not to express himself wrongly. Thoughts did not tumble out, they were shaped and examined before being voiced. He considered what he was about to say the way a mother inspects her small son's costume before introducing him to company.

"I'm glad you're running the outfit, Sam. That's fitting. It does me good to know. We taught you. Your dad, and Jake, and me, and all the men. You know the outfit and the work. You know it's the outfit and the work that matter. Spencer Butterfield just owns the outfit; we have the use of it. We take care of it for ourselves. The work is our boss. Preachers try to tell you heaven is where you sit around on a cloud and play a harp. I know better. For me it's the Rocking R. For me it's good horses to ride, good men beside you, and plenty of grass for the cattle."

Sam knew that all of the hands were not as devoted to the ranch or the work as a way of life as Tyler Taylor had been, but he felt that there was a level of traditional loyalty to the brand, and pride in the performance of their jobs, higher than you might expect to find elsewhere. On the Rocking R it was the land and livestock that were served, not the owner, and that gave the men a sense of independence and freedom, rather than servitude. But he reminded himself of what Jerry Whalen had said about the fifty stolen steers being worth more than his salary for a year. A powerful temptation.

Luis Pardee was not in his camp on Elk Creek, so Sam left a note and drove south to check the range conditions. The road made a right-angle turn when it reached the fence around the big pasture where the fillies ran with their eunuch stallion Barney. It was a rough, rocky section of the ranch, short-grass country where the black volcanic rock called malpais was never far beneath the surface and often right on top, forming lakelike patches of hardened lava where nothing grew. But where it did grow, the grass was nourishing and full of minerals that strengthened bone and muscle, hardened hooves, and kept the young mares as sleek as seals. Sam knew that this range was underutilized. He knew that there was a growing market for well-bred horses. If only he could get Butterfield to see that the horse operation on the ranch could be expanded into a profitable sideline. If only he could get Butterfield to see things his way.

As he drove along the fence, the band of fillies appeared on the skyline ahead, and he slowed to watch them spill over the crest and cascade to the flat below. The young horses were dark-colored bays and browns, and they ran nimbly on slender legs. Behind them trotted the elderly gray: Barney. The old gelding came stiffly down the slope as the fillies swooped and circled out over the plain. When they saw the blue pickup, they veered away and stopped, raising their heads to stare for a moment, and then they wheeled off with tossing manes. Barney moved methodically toward the fence where Sam had parked. Sam got out and watched him approach.

"Morning, Barney," Sam said, as the old horse walked toward him at a dignified gait, arching his neck. When he reached the fence, Barney thrust his head over the top strand of wire and allowed Sam to scratch him under his chin. Sam looked him over and saw no cuts or scrapes. Barney rubbed his head against Sam's chest and did not notice a shiny bay filly who was letting her curiosity get the better of her fear and was coming up behind him. Sam watched the filly as he rubbed and patted Barney. She was small and fine-boned with a classically shaped head and large dark eyes. She widened her eyes and flared her nostrils as she drew nearer. When she reached Barney's hip, she stopped, too shy to come close enough for Sam to touch her.

"Hello, lady," Sam said quietly, but at the sound of his voice the dainty little horse spun about and dashed toward where the herd of fillies stood. The movement triggered the band into action, and they scampered, kicking and squealing, in a wide arc toward higher ground.

"Go along, Barney," Sam said, giving the old gray a final pat. "Look after your harem."

Barney turned and trotted away with dignity. Sam sat on the fender of the pickup and watched him go, remembering when Barney had been young, before a thoughtless boy had "cooked" him, burned him out, by treating him as though he were a motorcycle and running him at full throttle until he collapsed. Since then Barney had been a wheezing asthmatic with only wind enough to trot sedately, but he was the nucleus of the band of fillies, and he was proud. The irony of it was, Sam was thinking, that if Barney had not been such an honest horse, he would not have been wind-broken. If he had not been so willing, he would have cheated and not given everything he had. He could have protected himself by holding back, but that was not in his nature. Old Barney, well, he had a good life now, and someday, maybe, there would be more fillies on the ranch than there were now. Maybe they would really get into the horse business, with leggy Thoroughbreds to train as polo ponies, and muscular Quarter Horses for rodeo roping. That was Sam's dream, and whenever he indulged in it, he thought back to the time he had spent in California training horses for polo on a ranch belonging to George Hickam.

Hickam's money came from oil, and a lot of it was spent on horses. He supported racehorses, show horses, and just plain pleasure horses, as well as several strings of polo ponies. Sam's job was to school the young polo prospects and serve as captain of Hickam's polo team. He was expected to play the young horses until they became reliable enough for his boss to handle, and to feed the ball to Hickam often enough during a match so he could score a few goals. The really fine horseflesh made up for some of the more trying aspects of the job for Sam. There had been many memorable horses.

Like Hardpan, Sam was thinking. I named him Hardpan because early on you could tell that he had bottom, he could stay. You could tell by the way he jumped out at the least little encouragement that he really enjoyed polo. At first he was just another dark-brown colt who bounded when he galloped, and lunged into turns, changing his lead a half stride late. He was bigger than most. Some said that he was too big for polo, but I liked the way his head was set on his neck, and the look in his eyes. It took me a while to get him collected, he was so interested in everything that was going on around him that he didn't always pay enough attention. But by the time he was ready for his first light scrimmage, you could tell he was going to be special just by how he watched the game and the way he moved under you. Nothing ever pleased him more than for you to really get into a shot and send that hard wooden ball whistling down the field in a rising drive that meant there was going to be a race. He could tell at the crack of the mallet head against the ball that it was a solid shot, good for distance. I would know by the shock that traveled up my wrist, but while I was still pulling the mallet through the swing, before I had gotten down to make a race out of it, Hardpan would have gathered himself and stretched into that all-out "I came to play" stride of his, and away we would go. If the ball drifted as it sailed, he would slide over with it, pounding along our right of way and never letting another horse and rider slip in and steal the line. If the next shot was to be at goal, he would bring us to the ball at the perfect angle.

I remember once at Broadmoor, when we were chasing a long lofting shot toward the goal all by ourselves, hearing the announcer tell the crowd, "Howard will have to slice his next shot." No, I thought, no, I'm not going to have to do any such thing. You just watch. And Hardpan sideslipped over, easy as you please, at a dead run and brought us to the ball at a perfect straight-in shot for a score. We swept between the red and white goalposts just after the ball did, and Hardpan slowed to a canter and turned back toward the field. All the way up to the center of the field he did his little rocking-horse lope, turning his head this way and that, looking at the crowd almost as if he were saying, "Isn't this fun? I'm having a grand time."

He didn't like to be rated down when he was going fullblast because he seemed to think that he should always be the first one to the ball, no matter what; but when I figured it was best, I could always turn him away to put us where I thought the next shot was coming. If I knew that the player on the ball at the moment had a habit of bringing the ball around, instead of backing it, I would steer Hardpan over toward where I thought the next shot was going to come. He would toss his head and look toward the action, telling me he thought we belonged in the thick of things, but when the white ball squirted out in our direction, he would pounce on it with glee, and away we would go. When I'd back a ball away from our goal, Hardpan would set himself up to turn away from the side where I had hit the ball. He thought that we wanted to go the other way, so he would start to turn. If I saw a player from the other team bearing down on the ball I had just backed, I would have to straighten Hardpan out and keep him going toward our own goal. He always let me know that he didn't think much of defensive play, but he would go on in case we had to back it again.

His game was the charge, the bumping and riding off, shoving opponents away so they couldn't make a shot, lunging out of a mix after the ball was tossed into play. He was never one for cautious, conservative tactics, and if you let him, he would change your style of play. Where I might be inclined to let an opponent take a shot, figuring to steal the ball from him afterward, Hardpan would give the opposition nothing. He wanted that ball *now*, not later. I think he was the only pony I ever played who enjoyed the game as much as I did. He liked it best when really good players were on the field. We had to put up with George Hickam. He owned us and paid us to play so he could play with us. I put up with the pudgy oilman, but Hardpan wouldn't. Some days George would invite his friends out for a game, and that was godawful. They would gang up on the ball and beat at it like they had found a snake. Hardpan would dance and wring his tail in irritation. I would keep us out where it was safe, and Hardpan would rage. He never understood, the way I did, that Hickam owned us.

But when we were in real competition at the high-goal tournaments, he came into his own. Then there were no knots of players bumping into one another in confusion, just long lofting shots sailing up the field and lots of turf to cover. With only good players on the field, it became a different game. We could count on them to stroke the ball well and stay spread out. The colors of their jerseys would be stretched in a long line: four dots of one color with four dots of another, man to man way down the field, wheeling and sweeping back and forth. The white ball would skim the green grass or rise against the blue sky at every crack of a mallet, and Hardpan would be in heaven. He seemed to want to be at both ends of the field at all times, everywhere at once. And he made you a better player than you really were.

Most horses don't like to meet a ball coming at them. Their myopia distorts that hard white blur flashing toward them, and they tend to duck off. Not Hardpan. Even on a penalty shot, when we had to stand flat-footed behind the back line, leaving the goal open until after the ball was hit. At the sound of the mallet and ball making contact, he would bound into the path of the ball and let me slam it aside, or he would take the shot on his shoulder to prevent it from going in. He dumped Hickam once doing that. Old George had watched me play Hardpan and asked me if I thought he could handle the brown horse. Well, Hardpan wasn't tough to handle, he had a velvet mouth, but you sure as hell had to ride him. I wasn't about to tell the boss that I didn't think he was up to it, so he said he would try him. He took Hardpan the next Sunday and was behind him all the way. He just camped on the big horse and held him back for almost the whole first chukker, and then committed a foul by stopping where he shouldn't have. An open goal penalty was called against us, so we lined up behind the back line to let them have a free shot. I guess George was just sitting up there watching when the ball was hit. I was on a pretty good young horse, and I made him jump out, but Hardpan came from the other side of the mouth of the goal and got there ahead of me. He was there, but George Hickam was on the ground at the back line. The ball hit Hardpan on the chest and bounced to one side. George never asked to ride him again. You wanted to be well screwed down into your saddle, and thinking ahead, when you had a leg over that horse.

Hardpan even enjoyed practice. Most ponies just put up with practice and conditioning, but he seemed to relish them. During the week I would keep him legged up with roadwork and solo stick and ball practice. Instead of loafing through it in the bored half-hearted way the others did, he would show off. When I would line him up for a nearside back shot, he would collect his stride and float toward the ball, so that the saddle didn't rise and fall. As I got ready for the stroke, he would shorten his stride just a bit, and when I shifted my weight to start the swing, he would drop his left shoulder as he changed leads. As the mallet came down, his weight would be added to my swing, and there would be a lovely, crisp "whack" that meant the timing had been perfect. Hardpan would reverse his leads to recover and turn away, nodding his head and flicking his tail, as if in approval, up against the bit, ready to do it again. It didn't seem to bother him that there was no audience for his performance.

Even the dull routines of road- and ringwork seemed to please him. He would rock along like a metronome, and sometimes he absorbed the shock so completely I had the feeling that he had discovered how to canter without touching the ground. I once saw Bill Robinson dance in a movie, and he floated like that. He looked as though he was only allowing his feet to touch the floor, and if he chose not to allow it, they would sail soundlessly through the air. Hardpan could make me think that he only allowed his hooves to come in contact with the ground. Tap-a-tattat, tap-a-tattat, we would float along with a loose rein until it was time for some figure eights, and then he would turn into twinkle toes. Reversing his leads, he would flash his black hooves in exaggerated flurries and dip into each turn like a tango dancer. When I judged that he had had enough, we would go back to the barn slack-reined at an easy walk. Most ponies come home on the bit, jigging urgently, anxious to be cooled out and back in their stalls. Hardpan always walked, swinging his handsome head from side to side, taking everything in and totally relaxed.

But his relaxation left when I turned up at the stables in white pants instead of Levi's. Those whites meant that we were going out for the real thing, the only thing that mattered. Polo was a grand game to me and, for a while, a good way of life. But polo was more than a game to Hardpan, it *was* life.

Sam drove back to headquarters depressed and uncertain. As he was filling the pickup's tank at the gas pump, he saw Lucy hurrying down toward him from the house. He sensed that something was wrong, and as he took her into his arms he felt her tremble.

"What's the matter?" he asked urgently.

"It's all right now," Lucy said, pressing her cheek against his chest. "I'm so damn glad you're back."

Sam led her to the house, where she poured him a cup of steaming coffee and told him that shortly after he had left that morning, and the rest of the crew had gone about their work, she had heard a piercing shriek from the cookhouse. She froze for an instant, and then without consciously realizing what she was doing, she grabbed a thirty-thirty carbine from the gun rack and dashed across the yard. The door to the cookhouse was open, and as she entered, she saw Pauline being bent backward over one of the trestle tables by a man whose back was toward her. She could see that the man had one hand over Pauline's mouth. As the Indian girl struggled, Lucy shouted, "Stop that!" and raised the rifle to her shoulder. The man turned his head at the sound of her voice, and she saw that it was Hank Ivy.

"Let go," Lucy demanded, and Hank stood up and dropped his long hands to his sides.

"Just having a little fun," he said. "No need to get excited."

Pauline was sobbing as she came to stand behind Lucy. Her face was scratched and bruised, and her dark eyes were glazed with shock. Lucy looked down the gun barrel at Hank. The tall man stared at the floor.

"No harm done," he said.

"Pauline," Lucy said without taking her eyes from Hank, "go to the house and wait for me. I'll be right there."

After the girl had left, Lucy, fighting to control her voice, said, "Get out of here. Get in your car and go. If you're here when Sam gets back, he'll kill you. If you make one funny move I'll do it myself. Now get!"

"What's the matter with him, Sam?" Lucy asked. "He must be crazy. My God, I actually came close to shooting him!"

"Jesus," Sam said. "What a lousy thing for you and Pauline. Is she all right?"

Lucy nodded and Sam took her in his arms again. He was proud of her, but all he could think of to say was, "You did fine."

Lucy shuddered and disengaged herself to go to the stove for more hot coffee. Sam went to the door and stood looking across the yard at the cookhouse.

"I never dreamed," he said and his voice trailed off. "I mean, Hank was always sort of a stud. He chased around a lot, but it was always just in fun."

"That's what he said," Lucy said. "But you know what really shocked me, made me so mad I was ready to pull that trigger? When I marched him to his car, he put one big hand on the door handle and looked at me and flapped his other hand and said, 'What the hell. She's only an Indian.' I couldn't believe my ears. I was so mad I couldn't say a word. He opened the door and got in and drove off before I could collect my wits. God, that made me angrier than I think I've ever been in my life. 'She's only an Indian.' What's the matter with him?"

Sam shook his head. "You're sure she's all right?"

Lucy nodded. "She's upset and sore from being manhandled, but she's all right. I think I'm more disturbed about the whole thing than she is. Oh, I shouldn't say that. I didn't get hurt. But it outraged me so. This is 1964, and there was that big goon sounding like George Armstrong Custer, for Pete's sake.

"Poor Pauline. She kept saying, 'Don't tell Martin. Don't tell Martin.' Over and over. I asked her why, and as she gradually calmed down a little, she told me that she's in love with Martin. She said that they both came from the same village over toward Window Rock and that she has known him all her life. She fell in love with him when she was fourteen, but he didn't feel he was fit to marry her because he is so much older than she and because he'd been in prison. He went away, and when she learned he was working here, she followed him. She's afraid that if Martin found out what Hank had tried to do, he would go after Hank and get in trouble."

"He likely would," Sam said quietly.

"Sam, how old do you think Martin is?"

"Well, he told me he enlisted right after Pearl Harbor. If he was eighteen or nineteen then, he'd have to be better than forty now."

"Pauline is just twenty," Lucy said, and paused. "I wonder what he was in prison for."

"Killed a man," Sam said.

"He *what?*"

"It was a fair fight," Sam said.

"You knew about it?"

Sam nodded. "Yeah, Red told me when he asked me if I had a job for Martin."

"You've known about it all along?"

"Yeah. I didn't tell you because I thought it might make you nervous."

"Oh, come on," Lucy objected. "You know I'm not the nervous type."

"I don't mean I thought you would lie awake nights," Sam said, "worrying about him killing one of us; just that it might make a difference in the way you related to him."

"I guess you're right," Lucy said. "What was the fight over?"

"Nothing much."

"Sam Howard, you have held out on me long enough. Now I want to know the whole story. What started the fight?"

"A bottle of booze."

"A what? You mean he killed a man over a bottle of whiskey? I can't believe it."

Sam nodded. "That's it. Red says that Martin got into the whiskey habit during the war. He saw a lot of combat in Italy, and when he came home he had a hard time settling down to reservation life. He started drinking pretty heavy. In those days it was illegal to sell whiskey to Indians, so he had to get somebody to buy him a jug. A stranger tried to charge him double what the bottle cost, and they got in an argument. When the white guy pulled a knife on him, Martin killed him with his bare hands."

"Good God!"

"They sent him up for manslaughter, and when he got out, he couldn't seem to settle down any better than before. He and his parole officer thought it would be a good idea for him to get off the reservation. The sheriff of Coconino County asked Red if he would find Martin a job over here, and Red called me. Red said that if I would give Martin a job, he could forget about reporting in as long as he stayed here and kept out of trouble. Well, he's been here five or six years, and he's one helluva hand. I just don't see any sense in talking about his past."

"Poor Martin," Lucy said softly. "And poor Pauline. She's really in love with him."

"Well," Sam said, getting to his feet, "they'll work it out."

"When we ship the steers, Martin will move back down here, won't he?" Lucy said in her low voice.

"I guess so," Sam said. "I want to get him working on some colts. Are you sure Pauline is all right? I could take her in to the doctor."

"No, she'll be fine," Lucy said. Then her eyes widened, and she lifted one hand to her mouth. "My God, Sam, I just realized something. That rifle I ran Hank off with. I just took it out of the rack. It wasn't even loaded."

"I know," Sam said. "But Hank didn't."

In the afternoon Will Michaels rode in at headquarters, leading a horse with his bedroll tied on it.

"Jake said you were going to be needing me," he told Sam. "Said I should come on down and stay till it's time to gather the bulls. Said he didn't want me riding around up there while Mr. Pardee was looking for rustlers 'cause I might do something dumb and get shot."

"Well," Sam said, "there's plenty for you to do here. Put your gear in the bunkhouse, and ask Lucy to feed you."

After stripping his horses and turning them out, Will said, with studied casualness, "You know, if I was aiming to doctor our brand, I'd just take a running iron and make a circle out of the rocker under the R and then burn in some spokes so as to make a wagon wheel out of it."

Sam Howard watched as the boy concentrated on drawing a Rocking R in the dirt with a stick and then converting it into a wagon wheel. The end result looked very like the photographs Red had given him. He knew that the only person beside Luis Pardee who had seen the pictures was Lucy.

"Where did you get that idea?" Sam asked quietly.

"Well, it just figures," Will said.

"You mean you just made that up?"

"Sort of. Not much else you could make out of it."

"Who told you about running irons?" Sam asked.

"Well," the boy said, "actually it was Jake. He told me about how they used to doctor brands in the old days. Not that he ever did any rustling, you understand. He just knows about how they did it."

"Did he tell you about the wagon wheel?"

"Well, I guess he did," Will said reluctantly. "I guess that's where I got the idea."

"Did Jake draw it for you?"

"Sort of," Will said. "Yeah, I guess he did. Mr. Pardee seemed real interested when I showed it to him. I met him on the ride down here. We visited a while. I drew him that wagon wheel around a Rocking R, and he got real interested. Asked me lots of questions about Jake and why I thought Jake was sending me down here and what Jake was going to be doing. Why do you suppose he did that?"

"No telling," Sam said, but as he gazed out across the horse pasture he was asking himself that same question and many more.

Could Jake have had a reason for wanting to work the steers east to be counted? How did Jake know about the wagon wheel brand? Had it been his idea or Jake's to send Will down to headquarters? Jake knew every gulch and gully on the ranch. He could easily have driven off a few steers at a time and hidden them. Whoa, now. Wait a minute. It could all just be coincidence. Cowboys are always inventing ways that brands could be altered. He had done it himself. He remembered Jake showing him how the old XIT brand had been turned into a Star Cross in a famous case years ago, and how he had doodled around with other brands, converting them. Jake could have just stumbled on to the wagon wheel. Besides, Jake just could not possibly have had anything to do with stealing the steers. Anybody but Jake. But Pardee didn't know Jake, and he had asked Will a lot of questions about the old-timer. If Pardee got it in his head that Jake was involved with the rustling, would he be apt to shoot first and ask questions later? That was what they did down on the Magdalena Ranch.

"Will," Sam said, "tell Lucy I'm going up to get Jake. I should be back by suppertime. You hold the fort while I'm gone."

"Sure," Will said earnestly. "You can count on me."

13

SAM FORCED THE RATTLING PICKUP over the rough road faster than he ordinarily would have because he felt an urgency, an ominous sense that Jake was in danger. Why would Pardee have questioned Will so closely about Jake if he was not suspicious that the old cowboy was involved in the rustling? I should have brought Jake down to headquarters the minute I turned Pardee loose up there, Sam told himself. His mind seized on "should have," and he remembered other times when he wished he had acted differently toward Jake, times in his boyhood when he had teased and tormented Jake. He recalled the fine times they had had together, and the pride they had felt in accomplishing the difficult and dangerous. He surprised himself by smiling over the memory of a minor incident, an unimportant moment in a time long ago, which came so clearly to mind that it seemed more important in recollection than it had when it happened.

Jake's horse had left him afoot miles from camp, and when Sam saw the horse, without Jake in the saddle, he had been alarmed. A horse loose with the saddle on could be serious. The cowpony, a chunky bay named Peanuts, was trotting toward Sam, carrying his head daintily to one side to avoid stepping on the ends of the dragging bridle reins. He stopped to graze, and Sam decided to catch him and backtrack the horse to find Jake. Just as he made that decision Peanuts raised his head and looked back the way he had come. Jake Scott limped into view, and the horse trotted on. Sam hid behind a piñon, thinking that it would be fun to let Jake follow the horse a little longer. Peanuts passed Sam, still carefully trailing the reins clear of his feet, and stopped again to snatch a few clumps of golden grass. Jake came by the tree Sam was behind, walking awkwardly, swearing in series.

"God *damn* you!" Jake muttered. "*Double* damn you! I'm gonna have me a new pair of chaps made outta horsehide after I catch you. You mean-natured, stump-sucking, hammer-headed, ram-nosed, ewe-necked, goat-withered, pigeon-toed, one-gutted, cat-hammed, cow-hocked, rat-tailed, ill-mannered sonofabitch. On second thought, after I get through with you there ain't even gonna be enough hide left for a pair of gloves."

Sam rode out from behind the scrubby tree and said, "Peanuts ain't cow-hocked. You can see that plain."

He was struggling unsuccessfully to suppress a grin as he rode up to Jake.

"Not one word outta you," Jake said. "Not a single, smart-aleck word. Just go catch that contrary bastard, and don't give me any lip."

A golden eagle glided on a thermal in the infinite sky off to the east as Sam bounced along the road that was not much more than a track. The great bird soared solitarily, with the primary feathers at either end of its seven-foot span of wings spread open like fingers. The eagle seemed low to the ground, but Sam knew that it was just beyond where the tableland of the plateau dropped off abruptly for a thousand feet into wild canyons and rocky draws. He remembered when he and his father and Jake had hunted down the last of the wild cattle in that area, known as Cottonwood Canyon, and it had been fenced off from the rest of the ranch. Catching the feral cattle had been a bone-bruising ordeal, but it had also been part of Sam's passage to manhood. They had packed in enough supplies for a week and camped by a spring at the bottom of the drop-off in a grove of ancient cottonwood trees. Two stout red mules, Nip and Tuck, had carried the supplies in and dragged the wild cattle up out of the canyon after they were caught. All of the cattle but one.

That one was a fierce renegade bull that they had gotten ropes on twice, but had not been able to hold. Bob Howard judged him to be about eight years old, and he bore neither earmarks nor brand. The dogs, Spud and Cindy, had jumped him the first day they worked the canyon, but the bull had eluded them.

Jake got a loop on him two days later, but the sixteen-hundred-pound outlaw charged Jake's horse and knocked it down. The bull was still dragging Jake's rope two days later when Bob Howard caught him, only to have the honda in his rope part when he tried to snub the enraged animal to a tree. On the evening before their last day in the canyon they made plans to ride their best horses and stick together the next day, in one final attempt to capture the bull.

"Let me see that hand of yours," his father said to Sam.

"It's all right," Sam said, not wanting to admit at sixteen that he was not tough enough to cope with a rope burn. "I greased it, and I can wear a glove."

Bob examined the damaged palm of his son's right hand. "Well," he said, "it's a long way from your heart, but quick as we get home you get your mother to put some of that bag balm she uses on the milk cow on it. That's the best medicine there is for a burn like that. What horse you aim to use tomorrow?"

"Gotch," Sam said.

"Well, for Christ's sake, watch him. You let him get steamed up and he'll run off with you."

Sam nodded, but he knew that he would not be cautious. He was determined to be the one to catch the wild and wily bull. If any horse could catch him, it was Gotch, a jittery Thoroughbred Sam had traded for at the county-fair rodeo. He was named Gotch because his right ear had been damaged, causing it to droop during the rare moments when he was relaxed. The nervous gelding had been raced and had never gotten over the conviction that whenever he was mounted he was expected to run at full speed. Sam loved the finely drawn blood bay for his fleetness and for the way he gave everything he had without reservation. It had taken the boy a long time to calm Gotch and quiet his apprehensions, and an even longer time to train him to a curb bit and loose reins. The horse's tongue had been terribly scarred by a twisted wire snaffle, almost cut in two, but Sam had patiently rebitted him until he was very light-mouthed and responsive. Responsive, that is, until he became caught up in running and switched off his mind. Once that happened, he lost all memory of training and simply ran.

Bob Howard did not approve of Gotch, not only because he was a runaway, but because he was too thin and highly strung, and because his legs were so light-boned that he would surely break down under ranch work. But he knew how Sam loved Gotch, and he remembered how many times in his own life he had made a fool of himself over a horse. As his son had gradually calmed the skittish bay and partially relieved its anxieties, Bob began to appreciate the horse more and to admit that maybe an ex-racehorse might have some use as a cowpony.

"My horses are all plumb wore out," Bob said, "except for Captain. You could pull a wet saddle blanket off that big, homely sonofabitch every day for a month, and he wouldn't show it. Guess I'll ride him."

Captain was a deep-chested sorrel that Bob had made a point of adding to his string after the horse had proved too mean and tough for any of the crew to handle. When the third cowboy in a row had given up, Bob took Captain on because in his late thirties, which he considered his prime, he did not believe that there was any horse he could not handle. He did not trust the coarse-headed horse, with the white rims showing in its eyes, but he respected the strength and stamina of the big horse, and when he stepped up into the saddle, he let it be known who was in charge. Captain tested him regularly by bucking whenever he got the chance, by trying to run under low branches, and by never missing an opportunity to shy violently from the slightest threat, real or imagined. Bob punished him with spurs and lashing reins, but always from the saddle, never from the ground. Captain would acknowledge the chastisement by showing even more of the white around his hazel, almost yellow, eyes and by blowing defiant, rolling snorts. The horse was durable, but untrustworthy; strong, but dangerous; indefatigable, but exhausting to ride.

"He's seventeen hands plus," Bob Howard often said. "Seventeen hands of horse, plus a whole lot of pure orneriness."

"The Mouse is all I've got left," Jake Scott said. "The rest of my ponies look like they were sent for and couldn't come. Old Mouse takes good care of himself, and there's nothing he dearly loves like hunting these ladino cattle. I swear he can smell 'em."

Mouse was a little Spanish Mustang, evolved from the Andalusian horses brought to North America in the sixteenth century by the conquistadores. Like his progenitors he had only five lumbar vertebrae and eighteen pairs of ribs, instead of the six vertebrae and nineteen pairs of ribs the other horses had. In these respects he was similar to Arabian horses, ancestors of the Andalusians, but he had none of the other Arabian characteristics except endurance. He had a flat face and small crescent-shaped nostrils set in a small muzzle, which bore a thick mustache of dark hair across the upper lip. His ebony eyes were set wide in his head, and like his short ears were rimmed by black hair. He was a mouse-colored roan, except for a black stripe that ran down his backbone from mane to tail. According to the Mexican who sold him to Bob Howard, this primitive dorsal stripe signified that the horse belonged to a strain that "dies before tiring." Jake did not know whether it was because of the stripe, but he did know that Mouse was tough. The little grulla could clamber over broken ground all day and still stride home at a swinging pace in the evening. He obviously enjoyed his work, and loved bossing cattle. If they did not move freely ahead of him, he would reach out and bite them hard along the backbone. At fourteen hands and eight hundred pounds he was small, but he was as agile as a goat: a fine horse for catching mavericks in Cottonwood Canyon.

"First thing tomorrow," Bob Howard said, "we'll go up and rim around for a look-see. That bull is watering at night somewhere, and if he hasn't sold out and quit the country altogether, we'll find him."

"I came onto a salt lick yesterday," Jake drawled. "Lots of big tracks around it. They coulda been his. You know that draw where we saw all them rattlers,

Sam? Well, maybe three cuts beyond it there's a big slide. That slide uncovered some layers of salt in the sandstone. You can see the streaks of white in the red. Lotsa tracks thereabouts."

"I'm not about to ride Gotch in amongst snakes," Sam said.

"This is way past there," Jake said. "We can send Spud and Cindy out ahead to let us know if there's any snakes around."

At the sound of their names the two tired dogs got up and came to be petted. They were black and white border collies with enough mixed breeding in their background to give them the extra size and toughness that working wild cattle demanded. Bob Howard stroked their silky heads with his work-gnarled hands that were so battered he could hardly straighten his fingers. Sam looked at his own rope-burned hand and back at his father's callused claws.

"Oh, you're good dogs," Bob crooned gently. "Best dogs ever. You just been eating on the wild bovine."

The dogs squirmed with pure delight, and each time Bob stopped stroking their heads with his curled fingers, they rooted at his hands with their muzzles until he began again.

"You know," Bob said, looking into the lowering flames of the campfire, "I just don't see what more a man could ask for. We've got horses to ride, and dogs to help us, and wild cattle to hunt. I'm going to be about half sorry when we catch that old bull tomorrow. Once we get him out of here, and fence off this hellhole, we won't get to do this anymore."

"I ain't gonna miss it," Jake said. "I want to get back

up where there's a little level ground, instead of everything being straight up and down the way it is in here."

They were halfway up the trail from the bottom of the canyon before it began to get light on top in the morning. Sam was still a little groggy with sleep, and his rope-burned hand had stiffened overnight. It was very sore. He had torn a strip from his bandana and wrapped it around his palm before pulling on a horse-hide glove. He did not like wearing gloves because he could not feel the balance of a rope as well as he could bare-handed, but without the glove he had no strength in the damaged hand. He stroked Gotch's neck, but the nervous horse kept nodding his head and rolling the copper cricket in his low port bit as he climbed up out of the dark ravine toward the daylight above. Three quarters of the way to the top Bob Howard turned off the main trail onto a narrow ledge that ran along the face of the canyon wall. Sam watched his father urge Captain forward. The big horse clearly did not think much of the footing. Behind Bob came Jake on his slate-gray roan. Jake balanced his weight toward the wall, and let Mouse have his head. The little horse moved along freely, placing each black hoof precisely, carrying his head down low. Sam followed Jake, leaving room for Gotch to be able to see plenty of the trail ahead. The apprehensive Thoroughbred scrambled in some loose rocks at first, and then began to settle down and pick his way carefully. Spud and Cindy brought up the rear.

When the ledge widened and the drop-off into the

canyon became a little less steep, Bob Howard stopped and studied the draws and arroyos below. Jake pointed to the slide where he believed he had seen the bull's tracks. Bob nodded and squinted down at the chaotic web of scars etched in the canyon floor. Suddenly he stood in his stirrups and pointed. Sam looked in the direction his father was indicating, but he could not see anything unusual. Bob said something to Jake, who nodded and turned back toward Sam, and then Bob put his big horse over the edge of the trail and began sliding down the slope, sending rocks rattling and crashing toward the bottom.

"We've got him spotted," Jake said. "Your dad's going to get beyond him, and we're going to cut him off from this side. That way we'll have him between us."

Sam turned Gotch back the way they had come. Spud and Cindy crouched against the wall to let them pass, and then trotted behind the horses. At the bottom of the trail Jake left Sam and turned Mouse up a wide gully. Sam and the dogs went into the next draw, which was narrower. He slipped the leather rope strap off the horn of his saddle and built a loop in the heavy nylon. He stood in his stirrups and searched the trail ahead, holding his reins and the spooled slack of the forty-foot catch-rope in his left hand and the loop shoulder high in his injured right hand. All thought of the soreness in that hand was gone. Gotch sensed Sam's tenseness and began working his ears back and forth, trying to pick up a sound that would tell him what was about to happen. They moved at a trot, and the narrow draw was filled with the clatter of iron horseshoes against the rocky ground. Suddenly there was a crash in the brush ahead, and the bull emerged, coming straight toward them.

Gotch dropped his hindquarters and slid to a stop as the two black and white dogs hurtled past, racing directly at the bull. For a moment Sam felt that time had stopped. There was the cimarron, the wild one, unmarked by man, belonging totally and only to himself, emanating belligerence. Sam felt very vulnerable. Confronted by the wild bull, he could only feel how ridiculous it was that a boy on a frightened skinny horse, armed only with a nylon rope, had ever entertained the idea of capturing such a monster. The spell was broken when the bull saw the dogs coming at him and snorted, shaking his huge head, wagging the heavy horns, which thrust wickedly out above his uncropped ears. He drew one massive splayed hoof back in a short pawing motion.

"Got hooves the size of stove lids," Jake had said, and Sam saw that it was true.

Then, just as abruptly as he had appeared, the bull wheeled with remarkable agility considering his bulk and crashed back into the thicket of brush. A moment of confrontation and he was gone, with the dogs right behind him.

"He's coming back," Sam shouted, and leaned forward, cuing Gotch to do what he liked most: run. Run he did. Branches slashed at Sam's face and clawed at his jacket and slammed against his knees and feet. The draw curved and dropped away sharply. Sam felt his saddle sink as Gotch seemed to fall, catch himself, and fall again. The bay horse was leaping down the steep rocky trail, falling forward, catching himself, and leaping. Sam balanced, leaned forward, gripped with his thighs against the swells of his saddle, and was shoved back against the cantle at every jump.

"All right, Gotch," he thought, "if you want to run, have right at her."

Gotch was not running so much as he was falling, scrambling, and plunging down through the rocks. Each time the saddle dropped away beneath him, Sam had the sensation of being weightless, of floating. He took the shock of each landing in his thighs and let the impact travel down to his feet, which were deep in the stirrups. He still held his rope ready.

Suddenly the canyon leveled out, and Sam saw the wild bull ahead, backed against the wall, fending off the two dogs, who were taking turns darting in to snap at him when he turned his horns from one to the other. The bull did not seem frightened, only annoyed and irritated. When he saw the horse and rider coming toward him at a dead run, he ignored the dogs altogether, lowered his broad curly-haired forehead, and charged the horse. Gotch was running blind, and Sam knew that the horse would not see the bull before it hit them, so he reached up and jammed his left spur into the horse's shoulder. Gotch sprang away from the bite of the rowel. The bull had his head down so he did not see the horse leap aside, and only brushed his sixteen hundred pounds against Sam's foot as he passed. In one fluid motion Sam twisted to his left and threw the ready loop across his body past his left shoulder, whipping it down hard to make it spread open in front of the bull. As the loop went on, Sam dragged Gotch to a stop, rolling him back on his hocks and turning him to the left to follow the bull, while Sam paid out slack in his rope. By the time the bull reached the steep rocky grade and had to slow down, Gotch had caught up with him, and Sam was taking in slack. Without a thought about his injured hand he quickly stacked three dallies of the rope around his saddle horn and brought the bull to a stop. Before the animal could make up its mind whether to charge the horse again or to try to break the rope holding him, Bob Howard and Jake Scott came clattering up the canyon and put their ropes on him. They soon had him lying helpless on his side with all four feet tied securely.

Sam stepped to the ground and stared at the malevolent bull. It did not look so ominous now. Gotch was blowing hard, and trembling. Sam stroked the nervous horse, and murmured to him.

"Ho, Gotch, ho. Easy now. You did fine. Ho, boy."

But Gotch would not, could not, calm down. He panted and sweated. He rolled the cricket in his bit, making a whirring sound, as he shifted his weight from foot to foot. Sam went on patting his lathered neck and crooning to him softly. He knew that no other horse could have caught up with the bull the way Gotch had. No other horse would have come down through those rocks that way. The dogs had been able to distract the bull and hold it for a moment, but they would not have been able to keep him pinned against the wall of the canyon much longer. Only Gotch, in his heedless, headlong charge, could have caught up so quickly.

"We heard you yell," Bob Howard said, "and we were just coming over that hogback yonder when you came down through them rocks."

"You looked like a big old truck tire rolling down the draw," Jake said with a grin, "just bouncing and falling from rock to rock."

"And that was some kind of hoolihan loop you dabbed on him," Bob Howard said, shaking his head. "You overhanded it like you just naturally expected it to go on, and damned if it didn't. Then you made that green-eyed runaway swap ends like he was a cutting horse."

Sam tingled with pride, and went on stroking Gotch.

"Well," Jake said, "I guess we better get on with the dirty work. I've got my little saw here. I'll just take about six inches off the ends of his horns, and we can snub him up to that there scrub oak. We can go along home and come back for him in three or four days. By then he ought to be soreheaded enough from fighting the rope to where old Nip and Tuck can lead him outta this snakepit."

"I guess so," Bob Howard said. "I hate to have to come back, but there's just no way we could get him outta here today."

Sam looked down at the bull. It was having trouble breathing, tied down the way it was, and its sides were heaving. Sam remembered how the big animal had looked when confronting him.

"Dad," Sam said quietly, "let's turn him loose."

"What?" Bob Howard said.

"Let's just let him go," Sam said. "He's good for nothing but baloney. Let's just ride out of here and tell the fence crew to close the canyon."

Bob Howard peered at his son from under the brim of his sweat-stained Stetson, and turned to look at the bull.

"Well, Scout," he finally said, "you caught him. I guess you got a right to say what happens to him."

"Now you're talking," Jake drawled. "We just naturally had to catch him to prove we could do it, but that don't mean we can't turn him go if we want to. Besides, if we ever feel like we want him later, we'll just send Sam and Gotch down here after him."

Good times, carefree times, Sam thought, watching the eagle stroking its wide wings lazily to gain altitude. Jake had been part of so many events of his boyhood: that first beer in The Homestead, the first trip to the whorehouse, the broken leg when they were practicing for the rodeo and Sam's horse had fallen. So many milestones and memories involving Jake. It had been Jake who met him with the news of his father's death when he drove into the yard at headquarters after twenty-four hours on the road.

"He's dead, Sam. He fought it right up to the last, and then he just sort of relaxed and let go. The strength was gone out of him, but he gave a damn good account of himself."

Sam let the words sink in. He lifted his head and gazed toward Baldy's gleaming peak.

"He'll be missed," Jake said softly. "No telling what's gonna become of this outfit without him. There's not many people understand this kind of country the way he did."

Sam had known then what he had to do. When Spencer Butterfield arrived later that day and urged Sam to stay and run the Rocking R, he had agreed to, not so much because Butterfield was persuasive as because Sam knew that he had a tradition to carry on. The land and livestock needed him.

Now Jake needed him, and Sam knew how much he needed Jake.

14

JAKE SCOTT WAS CONTENT. He sat on the stump that served as his chopping block and watched the breeze ripple across the carpet of golden grass that stretched out before him. The grass undulated as the puff of air swept toward him, passed, and rustled through the trees at his back. The big pines groaned, the aspen hissed, and then there was only stillness. Jake was glad to be alone. He was glad too that his part in Spencer Butterfield's scheme was behind him. The more he had thought about it the less he had liked the idea of keeping Sam in the dark, but Butterfield had insisted that only Jake and Luis Pardee, who were necessary to the plan, could know what was going on. On Thursday when Sam had brought Jake down from the Bill Williams camp, all that Sam had said was, "The boss wants to talk to you."

When Jake knocked gently on the door to the old log house at headquarters, Spencer Butterfield swung the heavy door open and said, "Come in, Jake, come in. I need your help."

Jake stepped into the softly lit room and passed the taller man. This was a very familiar place to Jake. A large stone fireplace was set into the wall opposite the front door, with the mounted head of a longhorn steer above it. The steer's head was poised with the muzzle lifted and the ears forward beneath the seven feet of curving black-tipped horns. Navajo rugs hung on the walls and large leather chairs flanked the dark fireplace. Jake waited until Butterfield folded his long frame into one chair and flopped a hand toward the other chair before he sat down with his hat in his lap. He felt perfectly at home. He and Spencer Butterfield had met often this way in years past, and they were at ease with one another.

"I've got a long story to tell you, Jake," the older man said, stretching his legs out straight and studying the pointed toes of his boots, "and you're the only one I want to hear it. I can't tell Sam. He has to go on about his business because he might try some kind of grandstand play if he was in on it, and that could spoil everything.

"Let me go back and begin at the beginning. A few years ago some of my people began sending in reports about eastern gangsters moving into Arizona. At first I didn't pay much attention. So many new people were coming into the state that it seemed natural we would get a share of the crooks along with honest people. But then the picture began to look more ominous. I checked with some FBI people I know in Washington and they really disturbed me. It turns out that these hoodlums are all organized, not just individual crooks

— a gang — and they're getting into everything. The men at the top decide when it's time to move in on something new. At first it was just drugs and prostitution. Then they got a bunch of phony land schemes going and took control of a couple of banks. They've just about taken over the liquor business, and they're working both ways across the border. My friends in the Mexican government tell me they are running guns south and dope back up."

"Sounds to me," Jake said quietly, "like they're spread around all over, like cow shit."

"That's it. They're called the Mafia and now they've decided to get into the cow business. I just will not stand for that. That's what I intend to stop. I'm going to let them know that they may be able to mess around with some things, but not cows.

"Here's what happened. I got a report that Oscar Bartley was in money trouble. Well, that's not exactly news. I've known Oscar for years and he has always been a great one for climbing out on a limb. When he started out he was just a gypsy cow trader working both ends against the middle. He'd buy some stock here, and sell them there, and run to the bank to cover the bad check he wrote to buy them with. He always lived from day to day, until the war came along, and then he made a bundle of money on black-market beef. He parlayed that into a feedlot–packing plant outfit down south named Genco. Just about the biggest in the country.

"Well, my information was that he had taken one big gamble too many, and he came up empty. He raised on a four-card flush and got called. That's happened to him before. He's turned two or three fortunes in his day. But this time, when he found the only bank that was willing to bail him out, it was one of the banks controlled by the Mafia. He was so desperate to get his hands on the money and salvage Genco that he didn't realize what he was getting into. Some of my people have worked their way into Genco and they tell me that the mob has taken over. They've paid off meat graders, brand inspectors, and the local law. Stolen cattle are coming in there, being fed out, killed and shipped out in boxes as steaks and hamburgers. You can't identify a hamburger. My people say it's getting worse and worse. I'm going to put a stop to it."

"Hmmm," Jake said. "How?"

"First, I talked to a friend of mine who's the state attorney general. He comes from an old ranching family. He already knew some of what I had to tell him, but he said that before he could send the state police into Genco he would need some pretty solid evidence to get a warrant. I told him to wait for word from me, but to start to work on the warrant. I had fifteen yearling steers brought from California, and my plan was to have their brands worked over and to plant them in Genco. The trouble was that nobody seems to know how to use a running iron anymore, so they botched the job. I had to dump the steers before they got some of my people arrested.

"When that didn't work, I had to figure a way to really get some Rocking R steers stolen, and that's where you come in. The people I have on the inside at Genco have set up a plan. They've convinced the mob that they have somebody up here who, for a thousand dollars, will put cattle down in the bottom of Cottonwood Canyon for them to pick up. The crooks can send a truck in on an old abandoned logging road from the east right to the bottom of the canyon. They'll bring in portable corrals and will expect to find about fifty head of steers waiting for them. I want you to persuade Sam to work the steers over to the Hart Prairie pasture and count them there. While they're gathering the Bill Williams country you cut out about fifty head and shove them over into Cottonwood Canyon. I know we've had it fenced off for years, the country being so rough and all, but there's water down in the bottom. They won't be there long."

"There's a problem there, boss," Jake said. "Sam's figuring on taking the steers south to the bull pasture to do his counting."

"You've got to convince him that it makes more sense to keep them in the high country. Take them over east instead of bringing them south to a lower range. They might not go back to the higher ground on their own and you would end up driving them both ways. Besides, it's almost time to bring the bulls in and we don't want all those steers tromping down the feed in that pasture. Think of all the reasons you can. You can make suggestions like that. I can't. I've got to stay out of it. I can tell him what needs to be done but not how to do it, you know that."

Jake nodded. "Not without you tell him what's

going on," the old cowboy said. "I don't see why you don't just let him in on your plan."

"No, Jake, I don't dare. You and Luis Pardee, the man who is coming up from Magdalena, are going to be the only ones to know. He's coming just to be sure that the rustlers don't try to pull any rough stuff, or take any more than we want them to. Once they haul those steers down to Genco and get them in the feedlot, I'll call the state police to go in and seize them as evidence. We'll put a few of those high-handed bastards in jail for a good long while. That should cure the Mafia of wanting any part of the cow business. I can't beat them in their rackets, but I can sure as hell make them wish they never thought about stealing cattle."

"Well," Jake drawled, "it makes pretty good sense to move the steers east to Hart Prairie and keep them on high ground. And it shouldn't be much of a trick for me to get fifty head into Cottonwood Canyon. I ain't been down in there for years, but I know right where the best place is to gap that fence. I was over there with the boy just a few weeks ago. Remember the time I took you down in there and showed you that spring?"

"I sure do," Butterfield said with a grin. "I didn't believe there was a part of this place that I hadn't seen, but you were way ahead of me. I had an aerial photo taken last week and it shows water and feed in the bottom where the old logging road ends. You just shove those steers far enough down in there and they'll stay a while."

"I've got to get rid of that boy when I go to make my move," Jake said. "I can't have him following me around asking questions."

"Send him down here on some excuse," Butterfield said and Jake nodded. "Tell him to come in for something you need. That will give you a couple of days. When the steers are in the canyon, tell Pardee. He'll have a radio with him and he'll send word to me. The truck will be up there that same day. You stay out of the way then. Pardee will make sure that they take the bait and go."

"All right, boss," Jake said, getting to his feet. "I still don't feel right about not leveling with Sam, though."

"I know you don't, Jake," Butterfield said, taking Jake's bony shoulder in his hand, "but if it will make you feel any better, I'll tell you this: He asked me to see if I could work out some way that he would share in the profit from the ranch instead of just working for wages. That's the first time I ever saw any indication that he was thinking about the future, the first real sign of maturity in him. If he's thinking ahead and settling down, I'll go him one better than that. I'll make him joint owner of the Rocking R. The doctor tells me my heart isn't in such good shape, and I want to make damn sure that somebody who cares will end up with this place. Somebody who knows how to treat it and keep it together.

"You know, Jake, I'm not going to leave my mark the way my grandfather did. There aren't any trails left to blaze. But this outfit can go on forever if it's handled right. Sam knows how, but I don't mind telling you, he's worried me."

"Sam's all right," Jake said. "Maybe he's been a little wild from time to time, but he's a good man. Sure, he's different from his father. Times have changed. Bob was willing to run this outfit for wages until he died, but Sam's been out and seen the world, and he's not as easy satisfied as Bob was. The Rocking R *was* the world to Bob."

"I know," Butterfield said quietly.

"Another thing," Jake went on, "a feller like Sam, with a lot of spunk, has a hard time being anybody's hired hand. He's got a lot of drive. He told me once that if he had his way, he was certain he could put us in the horse business, without hurting the cow operations, and get us to where a man wouldn't feel well mounted unless he was riding a horse with the Rocking R iron on it. I believe he could, too."

"All right," Butterfield said, "we'll give him a shot at it, but first I want you to help me teach these outlaw bastards that they made a mistake when they thought about rustling cattle."

"Oh, hell yes," Jake said, rearranging the arroyos of wrinkles in his face with a grin. "That's going to be purely a pleasure."

"And remember, Sam isn't even to get a hint as to what's going on. He might have to testify in court later, and I want to be sure that as far as he's concerned, these steers were stolen. What we're up to isn't strictly legal and it might mean trouble for Sam if he was party to it. He's going to have to front for the outfit and every move he makes has to be just right."

Jake rose and started for the door. He turned back

and asked, "What do I tell him you wanted to see me for?"

"I told him I was going to try to talk you into wintering in California on the San Benito ranch," Butterfield said.

"Ha!" Jake barked. "You should know better than that. I'm gonna take the cows to the desert same as always. You're not gonna make a irrigator out of this child."

"All right, Jake," Butterfield said with a smile. "But remember, you're always welcome."

Jake stood by the door, holding his wear-worn Stetson in front of his belt buckle.

"I know that, Spencer," he drawled softly, "and I appreciate it, but I want to look after my cows. And don't you worry, I'll have fifty steers in Cottonwood Canyon for them Genco Johnnies shortly."

Well, Jake was thinking, I've done my part. He went into the cabin and put a thin slice of leftover steak between the halves of a cold biscuit and came back to the stump to eat lunch. A chipmunk scuttled across the bed of wood chips at his feet, and the old cowboy tossed a bit of the biscuit on the ground. When the crumb landed, the little tan animal flicked its tail and froze; then it approached cautiously and picked the biscuit up with both front paws. Jake watched the black stripes along its back shift as it sat up and nibbled away, cramming crumbs into the pouches in its cheeks. Ringo, the roan horse Jake had kept in the corral to ride that afternoon, nickered toward the pasture where the other horses grazed. Jake planned to check a salt drop south of his camp after lunch. That morning, after he had seen Will off for headquarters, he had driven the steers all the way down to the spring in the bottom of Cottonwood Canyon, and had respliced the fence after coming back. Then he had ridden to Pardee's camp and told him that the bait was in place.

Luis Pardee rode along the fence above Cottonwood Canyon until he reached a juniper tree opposite a hogback that thrust out over the spring in the ravine below. He tied his horse to the twisted tree and loosened his cinch to make the horse more comfortable during its long wait. He lifted his rifle from its scabbard and slung a pair of black binoculars around his neck. After sliding his rifle under the bottom strand of the fence, he climbed over, stepping on the wires near where they were stapled to a post. He followed the ridge of the hogback, and once on top, he tested the direction of the wind with a shred of dry grass. Then he made his way to the end of the ridge, where he slipped behind a slab of sandstone outcropping and studied the basin below through the powerful glasses. He checked the spring and the grove of ancient shaggy-barked cottonwoods around it. The steers were there. He shifted the glasses and swept his view to the outer boundary fence and beyond, where the old logging road came out of the woods into a clearing. If everything went according to plan, the truck would park in the clearing, and a portable corral made of pipe would be set up just outside the fence. The fence would be cut, and the steers would be herded into the corral and up the truck's loading ramp. Once the steers were secure, the corral would be dismantled and hung in sections back on the side of the truck. The rustlers would return the way they had come, along the overgrown logging road, until they reached a good pumice road that led down to the highway. Pardee's instructions were to watch the operation and see to it that the rustlers took only what Butterfield wanted them to take. It seemed simple enough, but Luis Pardee was a perfectionist, and meticulous about every detail.

He settled himself and rechecked the setting of the scope on his rifle. He opened the bolt a crack to reassure himself that there was a round in the chamber, and ran through the estimates he had made of the distances to several locations in the basin below: a large rock beside the spring, a fence post, the edge of the clearing where the logging road ended, a patch of reddish earth just below his perch. He knew and trusted the rifle as he did his limbs. He had put thousands of rounds through it, testing different powders with various bullets. He knew that with a dead rest, such as he had now, he and the rifle could easily put ten bullets inside a two-inch circle anywhere he could see in the bottom of the canyon. The rifle was a .270. He had loaded and tested the cartridges for this job himself. They carried 150-grain bullets backed by 60 grains of number 7828 powder. This load would drive the sharply pointed bullet in a flat trajectory at three thousand feet per second and would kill anything smaller than a bull moose on impact. A well-placed shot would even kill a bull moose where it stood. He had no doubts about the rifle. The cross hairs in the telescope sight were set for 300 yards and Pardee was infallible at judging distance. He knew, without thinking about it, that with this load his bullets would be one and a half inches high at 50 yards, three inches high at 100, four inches at 150, four inches at 200, three inches at 250, dead center at 300, four inches low at 350, ten inches low at 400, and eighteen inches low at 500 yards. The fence post at the edge of the clearing below was 300 yards away and he had no doubts about the rifle or himself.

They should come today, he thought, but probably not until afternoon. He doubted that he would have to do any shooting, but if he had to, he wanted it to be a mathematical certainty that he would hit his target, so he rechecked the distances to the landmarks he had picked out. The sun was getting higher and warmer. By afternoon it would be hot in these rocks, but he was a patient man, and he had been hot before. His mind went back to that last assignment in South America. It had been hot then. The thought of that ordeal made him rub the palms of his hands down the outside of his thighs, a gesture which had become a habit when he was distressed. The episode was something he wanted to forget. He relaxed and made himself as comfortable as he could. He thought about that strange boy Will Michaels and their accidental encounter on the trail. When Will had proudly shown him how he would alter the Rocking R brand if he were a cow thief, Pardee had been startled, and had questioned the boy closely to make sure that he was ignorant of what was really going on. He was soon satisfied that Jake had not let slip any secrets and that Will did not know the real reason he was being sent down to headquarters. Pardee was saddened by Will's innocent determination to go to war. It seemed as though each generation had to learn that lesson first-hand at such an awful cost. He recalled his own eagerness to enlist after Pearl Harbor.

The sun was getting higher and hotter. Luis Pardee waited patiently.

Lucy answered the knock at the screen door and saw Will Michaels standing on the porch hat in hand. The boy's face was a study in contradictions: he was smiling in his unrestrained way, but his brow was furrowed and his wide-set blue eyes were squinted in concern.

"Howdy, ma'am," he said. "Sam told me to tell you he's gone to get Jake. Said he'd be back by supper. Told me to hold the fort. I'm not real sure what he meant by that, but maybe I can figure it out."

Lucy smiled. "It's just an expression he uses. Would you like some coffee, Will?"

"No, thanks. I got to tell Pauline I'll be around for a while, and get my bedroll over to the bunkhouse."

"Better tell her that Jake will be here for supper too, since Sam is bringing him down," Lucy said.

Will's eyebrows lifted. "That's right," he said.

"That's for certain. Wonder why Sam didn't tell me to tell her that?"

"Well," Lucy said gently, "he has a lot on his mind."

"Yeah," Will said, "he seemed kinda worried. He asked me lots of questions about Jake and Mr. Pardee. Well, I best go tell Pauline."

Lucy watched him stride toward the cookhouse, making his spurs ring with every step, and then she looked off toward the northeast where Sam was going. She knew that Sam had been worried about Jake ever since he had left Luis Pardee in the Elk Creek camp. Something must have happened to make him decide to go get Jake. Something threatening. Baldy glistened in the sun, solid and serene, but Lucy felt apprehensive.

Riding south from his camp, Jake Scott heard cattle bawling and knew at once what had happened because the sounds were not like those a cow makes when calling her calf or a bull would make when registering his claim to territory. He leaned forward, and Ringo pushed off on his hind legs and broke into a lope toward the fence above Cottonwood Canyon. Outside the fence stood three yearling steers with their noses tipped up bellowing toward scattered cattle in the distance. Jake drew Ringo down to a walk and roundly cursed the steers for their perversity. The yearlings stopped bawling and stared at the horse and rider with great interest and no indication of alarm. Jake waved his hat at them and swore some more. The three steers simply stared and stood their ground. Jake put his hat back on his head and turned them away from the fence by lashing at them with his rope. The three steers moved back a bit and stood watching as Jake opened the splice in the wire with his fence tool and led Ringo through the gap. They watched as he mounted and rode toward them. Not until he was within a rope's length did they suddenly wheel about in unison and plunge down the steep trail toward the bottom of the canyon. Jake followed them, leaving the gap open, because he knew he would be coming back that way.

"Of all the damn contrary, fanny-frying, ornery things I ever had to put up with," the old man grumbled aloud, "you three take the cake. You just naturally had to leave that cool water and sweet grass down below and come all the way back up here."

He lightened his weight in the saddle and let Ringo have his head. As the roan stepped over the rocks and carefully picked his way along the narrow trail, the steers scrambled on below him. Jake knew that he could not count on them to go all the way to the bottom of the canyon on their own; he would have to make the trip with them. Just when he had thought that this whole thing was over and done with, here he was back at it. From the position of the sun just over the rim of the canyon, he judged that it was just about two o'clock. As he neared the bottom of the narrow ravine, the heat grew more intense, and Ringo's neck was lathered where the reins lay against it. The sound of a truck motor echoed in the canyon, and Jake stopped Ringo at the edge of the grove of leafy cottonwood trees. The three homesick steers were drinking from a spring the trees surrounded, while the others grazed in the clearing. A big red truck came out of the pine forest blasting the silence in the canyon with the hammering noise of its diesel engine. The steers all lifted their heads and stared at the truck as it swung around in the clearing and backed up to the fence. Three men got out of the cab and began taking down sections of a pipe pen from the slatted sides of the stock rack. They set up a sturdy corral around the cleated ramp that led up into the trailer. When the sections of the pen were bolted together the fence was cut and tied to the open side of the pen. The men returned to the cab of the truck and brought out slender yellow buggy whips. They surrounded the steers in the grassy clearing and began driving them toward the corral. The yearlings milled in confusion for a moment and then rushed into the pen. Jake lifted his rein hand and turned Ringo toward the three steers by the spring.

"Hold on," he shouted. "There's three more here."

The men by the truck spun toward the sound and one of them ran to the cab and came back with a rifle held at the ready.

Sam Howard stopped his pickup in front of Jake's cabin and called out, "Anybody home?" There was no sign of smoke coming from the stove pipe, and the corral was empty, indicating that the old-timer was out "interviewing his cows." Sam pressed the horn button, sending three long blasts through the stillness, and then got out to squint across the waving grass of the horse pasture. He checked the shed beside the corrals and found only pack saddles. Jake was out horseback all right. Leaning on the top pole of the corral fence, Sam wondered what he should do next. Stay put, he guessed, and wait for Jake to come in. Off in the bright blue eastern sky he saw a speck which he supposed was a Forest Service helicopter surveying the timber. The sight reminded him of Red.

Old law and order, Sam thought, and without realizing that he was about to make an important decision, made one. To hell with it, he told himself, Butterfield may not like it, but just as soon as I get Jake moved down to headquarters I'm going to ask Red to start questioning the crew. Even if he turns up some answers I don't want to hear, I've got to know what the answers are. Luis Pardee may be Butterfield's solution to the problem, but Red Farnsworth is going to be mine.

He felt relieved for having made up his mind and decided to celebrate with a cigarette. Cupping the paper match in his hands to hide it from the wind, he took two deep draws and unconsciously shook the match out and bent it in two between his callused fingers. He watched the horses grazing in their fenced pasture and knew that they would spot Jake returning long before he would, so he decided to go to the cabin and warm up some coffee. He would be able to see the horses from the cabin door, and when they raised their heads he would know that Jake was coming home. Come home, Jake, Sam thought, hoping that the old cowboy would get the message. Come home now and let me take you where you'll be safe. Spencer Butterfield doesn't seem to believe that Luis Pardee has ever made a mistake. I'm not so sure. It could be that he has buried his mistakes. Maybe he knows Martin's method of getting rid of bodies.

Sam stood in the cabin door and stared out. The horses were grazing quietly, the sky was cloudless, and he noticed that the helicopter had moved to the south and was coming toward the boundary line of the ranch.

Despite the thrill he always enjoyed at being airborne, Red Farnsworth felt exposed and vulnerable behind the bubble of plexiglass that covered the cockpit of the little Forest Service helicopter. He watched the dark-green pines below for any sign of the old logging road a government timber cruiser had told him about. Frank Harper, the pilot, handled the noisy machine with confidence, and Red leaned forward against the web straps of his shoulder harness. They were over National Forest land to the east of the Rocking R, and Red was relieved to be doing something rather than just stewing over the stolen steers. He had always preferred being out on patrol to sitting at a desk, and this man-made hummingbird, which Frank could make hover in place, back up, or sweep slanting sideways across the sky, seemed the ideal vehicle for an aerial search. If there was a passable road through the forest, they would find it.

Red relaxed and let his eyes slip into half focus the

way he had learned to do when hunting. By not trying to see something particular he was able to notice more in general. He had learned as a boy that a big buck could stand perfectly still and make himself blend into his surroundings. If you concentrate on looking for antlers, all that you will see are branches, but if you look at the clump of branches collectively, you may notice a line or an angle that does not fit the pattern: a gentle curve, where everything else is jagged, might be the rounded tip of the buck's ear, a smudge of black where everything else is gray or green might be the cap of darker hair above his eyes. A smart old buck will freeze with his rack of antlers obscured by a bush of mountain mahogany and let you walk right by him, where a younger, less-experienced deer will bolt and give himself away. Red knew that you rarely killed a deer unless it made a mistake, and the satisfaction of hunting was in outwitting the wise ones. He had not hunted deer for several seasons, in part because he had lost the taste for killing and in part because the knee that had been shattered in the Pacific was not up to the walking anymore. Sitting in a pass waiting for a buck to wander by was not his idea of a hunt. But he kept his old rifle oiled and ready just in case. Someday it might seem right again. Some morning early Sam might come for him the way he used to when they were young, and they would slip through the woods as soundlessly as any Indians, gauging the wind and reading sign, letting their eyes take in the whole bush rather than looking at it branch by branch, letting the young deer panic and run, waiting for the patriarch to try to slip by undetected. Then when you did something smart, at the moment the big buck blundered, two lines would intersect, and there would be liver in the frying pan for supper.

So Red let his eyes take in the unbroken forest canopy, not looking for a road so much as looking for an indication, a change in texture and color, a straight line among the natural curves and contours. It had to be there, and he had to find it. He had to be able to go to Sam and say, "I know how those steers were hauled off the ranch. Now I'm going to find out who took them." Then Sam would have to listen to reason and let him get on with questioning the crew. Someone on the inside had to have played a part in the theft of the steers, no matter whether Sam was willing to accept the fact or not. But this was more than a simple case of a cowboy driving off a few animals at a time. Too many similar reports were coming in from all over the state. The whole picture was looking more ominous every day, with bunches of cattle missing from almost every county: thirty head here and fifty head there. Mattie had told him about the two strangers who had mentioned Genco. That might just be the key to the whole thing. Criminals were getting more and more sophisticated. In Jess Rainey's day things were simpler and more direct, but Jess never had one of these dandy whirlybirds to scout around in.

Just then Red realized that there was an unnaturally straight streak running east and west through the forest below.

Luis Pardee was watching the heat waves beginning to shimmer up from a large red rock on the floor of the canyon when he heard the truck groaning through the forest. Here they come, he thought, as he leaned forward and peered through his binoculars. From a relaxed reverie of his boyhood as a proud young *pistolero* searching for rustlers on the Magdalena Ranch, he brought himself alert and felt the excitement focusing his concentration. Now he would fulfill his part in Butterfield's plan and be able to go home. He had known how upsetting his presence was to Sam and knew that if their positions were reversed, if Sam had appeared on the Magdalena at Butterfield's insistence, it would have disturbed him mightily.

The truck drew into the clearing and was positioned against the fence. Pardee watched three men dismount from the cab and assemble a pipe corral. As he was putting his binoculars aside and picking up his rifle, he heard the sound of a helicopter and saw the machine bearing down on him just above the treetops from the east. Alarmed, he looked down into the canyon at the men loading the steers. They had evidently not heard the helicopter yet, but he knew that they would soon. He wondered how they would react when they did and tried to anticipate what his counter-response should be. At that moment a horseman rode out of the cottonwood trees. Pardee recognized Jake and groaned aloud. He heard the helicopter whining nearer, saw the glint of a gun barrel below, and without hesitating stood up in full view waving at Jake, shouting, "Go back! Go back!"

Jake drove the last three steers into the pen and was about to explain things to the man at the gate when a strange noise filled the gorge: WHOP-WHOP-WHOP-WHOP-WHOP-WHOP-WHOP. Ringo shied sideways, and Jake looked up to see a helicopter above. The machine hung there, unable to negotiate the narrow canyon, driving the sound of its rotor blades straight down in a pounding rhythm. Looking up, Jake became aware of a movement in the rocks at the top of the canyon wall. It was Pardee. He was waving at him to get away. Above the noise of the helicopter Jake heard one of the men by the truck shout, "We've been tricked!" He heard a shot and spurred Ringo, leaning forward as the roan horse leaped back toward the trees, rattling rocks. Just before they reached the trees, Jake felt a blow from behind. He gripped the saddle horn and looked up in time to see Pardee standing out in the open, drawing fire from the men at the truck. The last thing Jake saw was Pardee's body falling through the air toward the canyon floor. Then everything went black.

Sam was sitting on Jake's chopping block when he looked up to see Ringo walking slowly toward the corral. The sight of the body slumped over the saddle horn tightened Sam's stomach. He approached the roan horse cautiously, talking in low, soothing tones. Ringo let him ease Jake to the ground. The old cowboy was breathing, but his chambray shirt was black with blood all across the back. Sam carried him into the cabin and stretched him out on one of the beds. He was drawing water from the stubby pump at the sink when he heard the helicopter and ran outside. The machine lowered itself to earth, and the blades whipped slower and slower until they stopped. Red Farnsworth stepped to the ground from one side, and a man in a green U.S. Forest Service uniform came out of the other door.

"Christ, am I glad to see you," Sam said. "That goddamn gunman of Butterfield's has shot Jake. We've got to get him to a hospital."

Red stepped into the cabin, seeming to fill the single room. He went to the bed and took Jake's pulse.

"All right," Red said. "Get the stretcher, Frank, and the first-aid kit."

The man in uniform went out, and Red removed Jake's shirt and undershirt. The old cowboy's back was very white except for the streaks of dried blood and a blue hole under the right shoulder blade. Red took the first-aid kit, and while Frank unrolled the stretcher, he bandaged the wound. They carried Jake out to the helicopter and loaded him in. Sam squeezed in beside the stretcher, behind the two bucket seats, and the pilot lifted the machine gently from the ground. Red was talking into a microphone as they swept up into the cloudless chrome-blue sky.

"What do you mean, it wasn't Pardee?" Sam asked when he and Red sat down in the hospital cafeteria with heavy white mugs of coffee, after leaving Jake in the emergency room.

"Pardee didn't shoot him," Red said, tipping his Stetson to the back of his head with his thick index finger. "I saw the whole thing. I got the Forest Service to lend me Frank and the chopper so I could see if I could spot any way those steers could have been hauled off the ranch. We picked up an old logging road coming in from the east and followed it right to your fence at the end of a real steep gulch that has a spring in the bottom of it. South of Jake's camp and north of the windmill with the two black storage tanks. A narrow rough-looking cut."

"Cottonwood Canyon," Sam said. "It's been fenced off because it's so hard to gather."

"Well," Red went on, "we came right up there and saw a truck taking on around fifty head. Three men were loading the stock afoot, and Jake came riding out of the trees. I spotted Pardee up in the rocks on the top of the hogback. He had a rifle. I guess the guys stealing the cattle figured they had been set up when they saw the chopper. One of them took a shot at Jake, and since we couldn't put down in such a narrow place, I was getting ready to do some shooting myself, but Pardee stood up and showed himself, and they all began shooting at him. He waved at Jake to get gone. We couldn't get down low enough to do much good. Pardee got hit and fell clear to the bottom. The three with the truck piled in and took off. They didn't even take down their catch pen. Frank and I held back until we were sure which way they were going, and then we radioed ahead. The highway patrol will pick them up."

"You say you counted about fifty head?" Sam asked. "That's what I'm missing. How about those fifteen down in Pima County?"

"Damned if I know," Red said. "Maybe they cut these out after you made your tally."

Sam shook his head and rose to his feet as a young doctor joined them.

"He's all right," the doctor said, smiling. "Lost a lot of blood, but no serious damage done. The bullet caught a rib and slid right around it, so there is no lung damage. You can go up and see him if you want to."

Jake Scott was asleep when Sam and Red came quietly into his room. They stood at the foot of his bed, each holding his hat by the rolled brim just in front of his belt buckle. Against the starkly white sheets Jake's weathered face, except the pale upper part of his forehead, stood out in strong contrast. He was snoring softly. Sam and Red tiptoed out.

"Come on up to my office," Red said as they left the building. "I'll put in some calls and see what's going on."

"OK," Sam said. "I've got to call Butterfield, too."

But when they reached Red's office, there was a message saying that Spencer Butterfield would be landing at the airport within the hour.

"What do you want to bet that he knows everything that's happened?" Sam said. "He probably knows more than we do."

"It wouldn't surprise me," Red said with a grin.

The first thing Spencer Butterfield said after stepping down from his private jet was, "How's Jake?"

Sam and Red assured him that the old cowboy was going to be all right. The second thing he said, as Red drove them out of the airport parking lot, was, "I owe both of you apologies." Sam saw Red look up into the rearview mirror, and he twisted in the front seat to look back at his boss.

"How come?" Sam asked.

As Red drove to the hospital, Spencer Butterfield went over the whole story, explaining how he planned to have the Rocking R steers stolen and shipped to Genco, where they would be evidence enough to send many of the crooks to jail and get the Mafia out of the cow business once and for all. Sam listened with a mounting sense of outrage.

"Godamighty, Spencer," he interrupted, "you could've told *me.*"

"I should have, Sam," the rancher said. "I realize that now, but in the beginning I felt that I didn't dare. You see, I wanted everyone, especially the gang at Genco, to believe that those steers really had been stolen."

"Otherwise," Red said, "the case against them could be thrown out of court on grounds of entrapment or tainted evidence."

"Exactly," Butterfield said. "You two had to act exactly the way you would if the theft were a real one. Genco had to believe that they had a man on the inside at the ranch who was setting things up. They even made a payoff to Jake in a Phoenix bank. We're going to get them."

"But I've gone and spoiled it," Red said.

"You and that damn helicopter," Sam said with a grin.

"You haven't spoiled anything," Butterfield said. "You both behaved splendidly."

"I think I've wrecked the whole thing," Red said glumly. "I radioed the state police to stop that truck. Those steers will never get to Genco."

"Yes they will," Butterfield said with one of his rare smiles. "The state police were alerted ahead of time to let that truck proceed and to report on it as it passed a series of checkpoints getting from here to Genco. The last word I had was that they were right on schedule. My guess is that they think they got away clean."

"Well," Sam said, "I hope that's the end of that. This whole thing has been a nightmare."

"I know it's been hard on both of you," Butterfield said. "My people were watching at Genco, and the Mafia was watching you. They had a man on the scene to make sure that it wasn't some kind of setup."

"Who?" Sam and Red asked simultaneously.

"Your former friend Hank Ivy, Sam."

"I'll be damned," Sam said.

"You see," Butterfield went on. "If you had known what was going on, you wouldn't have been as distressed as you were, and that would have given us away."

"I'll be go to hell," Sam said. "You know, Lucy was worried about him."

Red stood up slowly and put on his hat. He looked down at Spencer Butterfield and said, "I'll get Frank to fly me back up to that canyon and see if we can land in the clearing where that truck was so we can bring Pardee's body out."

"Yes," Butterfield said, staring at the floor, "I'll take him home to Magdalena."

Red left and Sam leaned forward saying, "I still wish to hell you had let me in on your scheme. The way it was I was ready to suspect anybody, couldn't sleep, was working up a goddamn ulcer. When Pardee came I figured you must have thought I couldn't handle things. I was damn near ready to quit. I may yet."

Butterfield raised his head and nodded.

"I understand how you feel," he said. "Jake wanted me to tell you. I didn't think I should."

"Well," Sam said, "if I'd been in on it I'll bet Jake wouldn't be lying upstairs with a hole in him, and Luis Pardee would — "

"Stop Sam. Don't remind me. Luis was very important to me."

Sam hesitated, and then he knew that his anger was subsiding. At first, seeing Butterfield so defeated had made him feel strong, but now he was losing his desire to vent his frustrations. Like Red, he found that he could not bring himself to kick a man who was down.

"I have some papers here," Spencer Butterfield said, drawing an envelope from his pocket. "Look them over and sign them where I have. They make us joint owners of the Rocking R. I know you'll take good care of the outfit. Now I'm going up and see if Jake is awake."

Sam stared at the envelope as Butterfield pushed it toward him and rose from the table. He was still staring at it when the tall man turned and headed for the door.

Spencer Butterfield approached Jake Scott's hospital bed as quietly as he could, but the old cowboy's eyes opened, and the deep wrinkles around his mouth shifted as he stretched his lips into a wry grin.

"I feel like I been used hard and put away wet," Jake said in his gentle drawl. "I'm purely stiff and sore."

"You're going to be as good as new, Jake," Butterfield said. "Just take it easy."

"Only way I *can* take it," Jake said. "Any move I make hurts like hell. Even breathing."

"Well," Butterfield said, "the doctor says you'll be sore for a while, but not for long."

"Is Pardee dead?" Jake asked, and Butterfield nodded. "I remember seeing him fall," Jake said quietly. "He was one brave man. I guess if it hadn't been for him I'd be a goner for sure. Another thing I remember: I came to partway in a ambulance or something, and Sam was leaning over me. He had tears on his cheeks. He never cried when he was a kid."

"He told me he thought you were going to die," Butterfield said. "He was blaming himself for not getting you out of the way before the trouble started. He thought Luis had shot you by mistake. I told him the whole story. Told him it was my fault. Then I gave him some papers to sign — the ones that make us joint owners of the ranch."

"Good," Jake said. "There's nobody in the world

that'll take better care of the outfit. You can count on that."

"I know," Butterfield said in his low rumble. "I feel a good deal easier."

Sam Howard steered the car he had borrowed from Red out along the highway toward home. His spirits were soaring. It was one of the most beautiful days he had ever seen in his life. The sky was intensely blue, and the few little puffball clouds hanging above made it seem bluer by their whiteness. When he passed the patch in the barbed-wire fence, he laughed aloud and pounded on the steering wheel. "Damn fool," he said, and thought, I'm as bad as Molly with the porkies, and I guess I'll never change. I ought to have enough sense to quit and go home when the drinks get to tasting too good and going down too easy.

His mind was churning with plans, and he felt an urgent need to share them with Lucy. On impulse he flipped a switch on the instrument panel and heard the car's siren groan to life. The sound swelled and rose in pitch. The noise peaked and fell, wailing rhythmically, surrounding him until he felt that he was floating in a funnel of oscillating din. At first he felt exhilarated, and understood why Jerry Whalen was so fond of sirens, but the noise soon became oppressive, overpowering his thoughts, so he switched it off. He had plans to make. First, the bulls have to be brought in, then it will be time to ship the dry cows, and this year's colts need branding. When we wean and halter break the colts in December, we should set up more elaborate records of each stallion's get. Next spring it would be a good idea not to geld some of the best two-year-old horse colts and raise them as studs. If we're going into the horse business in a big way, we'll need more good stallions. No "if" about it, we surely are. We'll have to buy some breeding stock, but the foundation of the herd we are going to build on is already there: fine mares and sound, ranch-bred stallions. We'll bring in some Thoroughbreds and Quarter Horses. Lucy is going to be in heaven. And me? I'm going to have the chance to use what I've learned from all those good horses in my life. Now, remembering all those fine horses, I'll breed to make more like them and, in time, there will be others worth remembering. The horses buried in the aspen grove will be my models. We'll see the likes of them again, and some day the Rocking R iron will mean the best there is to be had in horseflesh.

Sam let his mind slide into a daydream:

"You say you're looking for a colt with real potential for high-goal polo? Well, right over here is a likely young horse. We call him Hardpan. He's still a little green, but he loves the game.

"Now, for indoor polo you want a smaller, handier kind. This little feller, Mouse, is a dandy. He's out of a Spanish Mustang mare I bought in Old Mexico, by a Quarter Horse stud. I played him myself last winter and he turned inside of everybody.

"This is Reno. He's by a Quarter Horse stud that has given all his get good steady dispositions. We're schooling Reno as a cutting horse, and he's coming along just fine. He'll be ready for competition next spring.

"Here's Gotch. He's a Thoroughbred and as fast as they come. No, we don't aim to race him. We use him when we're chasing fillies, and for breeding speed into some of our mares. Yes, he's a stallion, but we use him for ranch work. He's well-mannered.

"If you're interested in breeding stock I can show you our fillies. We have over a hundred head out on pasture with an old gray gelding just east of here. Fine fillies. Or if it's using horses you need, all these geldings in this paddock have been doing ranch work since they were three. That big sorrel? That's Captain, and he's just as stout as he looks. You could pull a wet saddle blanket off him every day for a month and he'd never show it. They're all good honest using horses, every one. Blucher, Sundown, Duke, Chigger, Harvey, Fudge, Monkey, Cyclone, Whiskey, Buck. All Grade A fine. We cull the three-year-olds heavy, and anything we keep for ranch work has to be special.

"This horse I'm riding? He's a dandy. His name is Rebel. He's ranch-bred. That's his full brother over there, the one the big guy in the black hat is riding. No, they're neither one for sale."

Sam shook off his fantasy, and unconsciously glanced toward Baldy to check his location. When he saw the turnoff to the ranch road, he looked in the rearview mirror, braked, and swung off the highway to be confronted by a barricade of dead limbs and brush. He stopped the car and got out, puzzled. From behind a juniper tree beside the road, a voice called out, "State your business!" Sam turned toward the tree and realized that the voice belonged to Will Michaels. A wide grin drew out the corners of Sam's mouth.

"Come on out, Will," he said. "The trouble's over. Let's go look to our livestock."